The Ulasiga

Glenn Parkhurst

ALL THINGS
THAT MATTER
PRESS

ISBN: 9780985006693

Library of Congress Control Number: 2012942206

Cover art by: Jensen DiGiulian

Published in 2012 by All Things That Matter Press

For my Mother and Father, words are insufficient.
I love you.

Acknowledgments

I want to thank all my little buddies who showed me that emotions do not have to be hidden and that unconditional life is electric. Without you, this story could not have been written. I would also like to thank Melanie and Donna for their work.

ONE

If it had eyes, the ulasiga would have opened them. Instead, it opened its mind. It felt something moving on the surface.

"Are you sure you want to use the cave," said young Csawi. "You know the stories."

Tsani looked at Csawi. "There have been no other Passings done in a cave. Everyone goes high up the mountain or beside the river. I want to be different. I want my name to be different. Besides, who believes those tales? Babies and children. We are men."

"I'm glad you chose me to be your witness. I promise to wait here until your time has passed. I will listen and remember your spirit words," said Csawi.

"As I will yours, when your time comes."

The two young men shook hands and Tsani bent low and entered into the darkness of the cave, a small torch in his hand. Inside the first chamber, Tsani looked at the blankets and water jugs along the stone wall. He wouldn't be using any of their supplies because the Passing required a fast. He got down on his knees and crawled through the next hole into the smaller inner chamber. Unable to stand in the low space, he made himself comfortable by sitting cross-legged in the center facing the entrance.

The ulasiga moved toward the wall of its lair deep underground, slipping into a fissure that led to the cave above. Stretching its gelled form, it oozed through cracks in the rock, some as thin as a hair. The leading end of the creature carefully tested every new turn and opening for deadly light while the major portion of its body remained in the lair. It continued to monitor the movement and probe for the brain activity of whatever moved above.

"Can you hear me, Csawi?" Tsani called.

"Yes," replied Csawi sitting outside at the entrance of the main cave.

"Then let the Passing begin."

Tsani looked at the walls to memorize the layout of the cave then extinguished the torch plunging the room into total darkness. He would have no contact with the outside over the next two days. Tsani watched as the daylight that filtered in through the small opening faded.

Tsani had begun the Passing, a ritual of the Aauete Tribe. He would stay inside the cave fasting for two days, then emerge and bring his visions to the elders for interpretation. These dreams would give him his man's name, making him a full member of the tribe. Many before had chosen the tops of mountains, under eagles' nests, beside raging rivers, or beneath the canopy of a giant oak. Tsani chose the cave.

Tsani remembered when he and Csawi had discovered the cave in early spring while exploring the forest. It had recently been revealed when a rock slide pushed the boulders from the opening. They explored it with torches made from hemp and dipped in animal fat. It had been small, only two chambers deep, but it served as a hiding place where the two could come alone and pretend to be great warriors. They claimed it as their special place, and believed they could feel the presence of their ancestors within.

They had made a pact to keep it a secret until they had used it for the Passing, hoping it would bring visions unmatched in the tribe.

Outside, Csawi waited beside a small campfire. He listened closely for sounds from within as he roasted small chunks of venison. Any words he heard from Tsani during the fast, he would bring back to the elders to help them unravel the visions.

Csawi stayed vigilant that night, even though he knew the visions would not come until the next day or night. He remained awake at the mouth of the cave, listening for Tsani, waiting for his voice.

Tsani chanted softly to himself in the pitch black cave waiting for the visions his elders said would come near the end of the second day. Tsani was sure he heard soft voices calling him. He knew it had to be too soon, but maybe that was proof that his would be a special Passing.

On the second day at sunset, there still had been no sound from inside. Csawi stood, leaning up against the rough rock wall to help him stay awake. He felt his eyelids sag as tiny dreams intermingled with his thoughts. He fought them even as his mind drifted along with the soft voices. In his dreams, the darkness inside the cave called to him. He saw the great chiefs standing on the far banks of the wide river. They beckoned to him to cross and join them for the hunt.

Csawi took a step toward them, but his knee buckled and the sudden movement woke him. He looked for the chiefs, still halfway in the dream, but saw only shadows formed by light from the rising full moon. The time of Passing was complete.

Csawi stood at the mouth of the cave and called to his friend. Only echoes returned.

"Tsani, quit playing. The time is done. Come on, let's go tell the elders."

There still was no answer from Tsani. Once again he felt the pull of the dark. It whispered to him, trying to draw him in. Csawi saw nothing, but felt a strange urge to enter the cave. He turned and walked back toward the fire to make a torch, but the fire had gone out. He turned back toward the cave. Should I go in, he wondered. Although the time of Passing had ended, he didn't know what custom dictated. What if his friend needed him? But why would he? He moved toward the pitch black opening. He felt his knees weaken and he bit his lip trying to erase the fear. He knew that even in the dark, he could feel his way through to the small cave and Tsani. Then he heard Tsani call to him, yet the voice sounded different from Tsani, deeper, more rhythmic. Once again the visions of great chiefs calling him returned. He moved closer to the entrance. He took one stiff step, then another. He stepped into the darkness. The barking of a nearby coyote snapped him out of it. The old stories of the ulasiga flashed through his mind. Csawi bolted back to the camp to find his father. He found his mother at the campfire with the other women. He skidded to a stop.

"What is it? Where's Tsani?" Csawi's mother asked. She stood from her seat.

"I need father. Where is he?"

"At the place of Maga," she said. "Why? You shouldn't disturb him."

Csawi turned and ran toward Maga's lodge without another word. He stopped outside the flap that covered the opening. Impatient, he stood there shifting his weight from one foot to the other. He heard the two men inside speaking. He wondered how to interrupt, something he had learned to never do. Finally, he could wait no longer. He called his father. "Denili, I wish to have words."

Csawi paced back and forth waiting for a reply. He could hear the two men inside talking. They would not end their conversation soon. Breaking from custom and courtesy, Csawi called again, louder.

"Denili, I wish words!" Csawi put as much urgency as he could into his voice.

The flap of the tent opened and Denili stepped out with his hand already in motion. Csawi flew backwards when the back of his father's hand struck him across the cheek.

"Puppies learn quicker and have more manners than you," Denili said. He looked down at his son who lay sprawled on the ground.

"Apologies, Denili. Tsani's Passing has finished, but he will not call out and I felt the spirits of the dark call me."

"Where is he that you cannot see him?" Denili laughed. He shared a look with Maga. Here was his child, trembling, afraid of the dark, even as his time of Passing approached. Would he be ready? Maga acknowledged Denili's disappointment with a wan smile.

"He used a cave we found for his Passing."

Denili's head snapped back around and Maga stepped up beside him to look at the boy on the ground.

"Where?"

"In a cave we found last year."

"Show us." Maga turned to Denili. "Get the others."

Csawi led Maga up the side of the hill and off the trail along the base of a tall cliff. He took him to the entrance and pointed.

"Tsani!" yelled Maga.

Silence from the cave.

Tsani's father, Tsegi, came up behind them and pushed by. Maga grabbed his arm. "Perhaps I should go first."

Tsegi jerked his arm back. "It is my son! I shall enter and see why he has not answered. And if it is Ulasiga Gvhna, I shall be the first to challenge him, the living night."

"Wait for the torches," Maga said.

Tsegi entered, hands feeling his way along. Maga stayed at the entrance waiting for the others, not sure what to do.

The small cave barely held Tsegi. Tsegi ran his hand along the wall until he found the small opening described by Csawi. He felt a pull, one that spoke of greatness and wealth. Tsegi resisted, remembering the words passed down through many years. He yelled for a torch.

Denili arrived with others carrying torches. He passed one inside. Tsegi snatched it and thrust it through the opening. A searing pain ripped through his head. The others outside fell to their knees, grabbing their temples, feeling the sudden stab. Then suddenly, it was gone.

Tsegi crawled through the smaller hole, to the inner cave. There, he lifted his torch, exposing the body of his son. The boy's face was melted away and his head was almost separated from his body by a bloodless cut. An arm was missing. It wasn't a ragged, bloody stump, like something chewed away by a predator. Rather, it was more like his arm had been melted away, bone and all. A trail of steaming liquid ran into a narrow crack in the cave.

Tsegi fell to his knees and began to wail, a cry heard all the way outside the cave and echoed across the valley. Minutes passed before the others could bring him out. Two men led him back to the village while the others stayed and began covering the entrance with boulders.

Tsani's body was left inside, given over to the living night, the Ulasiga Gvhna, the legend passed down through the tribe since the great sun god gave up half of its domain to the night.

TWO

Davy looked in the mirror and smiled. I'm not the smartest guy by a long shot, he thought. No sir, nobody will ever make that mistake. I'm not dumb either, he told himself, making an angry face in the mirror.

He looked over at his diploma hanging on the wall. He had finished high school just shy of 23 years-old. More importantly, he was able to live alone in a small apartment above a card shop.

Davy looked back at himself in the mirror. He rubbed his cheeks trying to remove the eternal baby face that came with him having Down syndrome. He pulled down at the corner of his eyes trying to make them look normal. He ran his hand through his black silky hair and watched it fall into place as always, straight down from center. He knew his looks caused people to hesitate just a moment when they saw him. He felt around his stomach, happy that at least he kept his weight down, unlike the other people like him that always seemed to carry several extra pounds. He worked extra hard to keep his weight under control.

He looked over at a map on the wall. The map showed city and state trails that ran in the foothills and up into the mountains that stood east of the city. Some were colored. Davy counted the ones that weren't. Those were the ones he hadn't hiked yet. Hanging next to it was the bus pass he used that carried him to the edge of the town so he could hike the local trails up into the mountains. Davy placed his finger on one trail he had colored green. As his finger traced the route, he tried to imagine hiking it now. He could see the blotches of paint on trees along the trail. He knew the green one was one of the city trails. City trails weren't too hard and usually had benches along them to rest. Davy laughed when he imagined a great mountain man like Davy Crockett, in his coon skin cap, sitting on a park bench. Davy was excited because Saturday he was going hiking and had picked out a trail already. It was the next to last one on his list. Davy went down his hiking list to make sure he had everything ready for Saturday. It was a long trail so he'd need a couple of snacks. He could buy them at the store. He checked his flashlight, whistle, and windbreaker. He usually took his time hiking, happy that he had all day. On this trip he would hike until the hands on his watch met at the top, noon, then turn to go back. He wondered if he would see as many families on this trail as he did on the other city trails. The people hiking were usually happy and smiling. Maybe he would find some different trees. He had seen the pine with the long green needles. He liked the white bark trees. Those were birch. He had looked that up on the computer. He wondered if there would be big boulders and places where the big trees fell over so he could play cowboys and Indians or Davy Crockett. As long as he didn't stray too far from the trail, he reminded himself. He didn't want to lose the ribbon of brown.

Davy paused for a moment and remembered back to the time when he had gotten lost. It had been during the early fall when he found himself off the path. He'd been looking at the bright leaves scattered about on the ground. He wanted to remember the shapes so he could look them up later and wanted to find a perfect one to take to his friend, Roberta. When he looked up, he didn't see any trees with his color marking it. In fact, he hadn't seen any paint on any of the trees. He looked for the brown dirt of the trail and couldn't see that. That had scared him so much his heart began to beat faster and he had to pee. He had looked wildly around to see if he could see something familiar. He looked around on the ground hoping to see tracks like he had imagined Davy Crockett would, but the leaf-strewn carpet hid any footprints. He had been about ready to scream for help when he heard a child crying. His pushed his fear aside and focused on the sound; followed it as it rose and fell, weaving his way between trees and around bushes. He didn't go far before he had found himself back on the trail. A small boy about seven, sat all alone on a rock, tears streaking his dirty face.

"Hello," said Davy.

The boy had looked up, sniffing and wiping his runny nose. He saw a man standing there with a big smile and that the man had been crying, too. Suddenly, he felt warm inside and it tickled. He had to smile. He wasn't scared anymore.

Davy saw the smile and eased back on the tickle he had sent, a talent Davy didn't understand and didn't like to talk about.

"You lost?" he asked.

"I was playin' hide-n-seek and when I came out I didn't see anybody."

"That's okay. I'm here. We'll find your mom and dad. Look," Davy pointed to a red splash on a tree trunk.

"This is the trail I'm on."

Davy pulled out his index card with the red circle and showed it to the boy. "If we follow the red we'll get home just fine."

"Look, there's another one," said the boy. He'd taken Davy's hand and pulled him down the trail. They had only gone about a quarter mile when they could hear voices shouting.

"Ryan!"

"That's me!" the boy had said. "Mom!"

Ryan took off down the trail with Davy right behind.

"Be careful! You shouldn't run on the trail," Davy called after him. Davy didn't run so well and the boy left him behind, disappearing around a corner in the path.

Davy rounded the corner just in time to see Ryan run into his mother's arms. The boy's father was bent over and yelling at him.

"What's the matter with you? Didn't I tell you to stay with us?"

Davy skidded to a halt, huffing and puffing. The father stopped in the middle of the next sentence and looked at Davy. Davy saw that moment of recognition in the man's eyes. He saw it on the face of every adult he had ever encountered. The man turned quickly to his son.

"Is this guy chasing you? Did he try to touch you?" he turned toward Davy. "Hey, you! What're you doing?"

Davy saw the anger building in the man's face, which was already red from yelling. Davy froze as he tried to think of what to say. He started to back up and caught his boot on a root. He fell to the ground on his back. Panic quickly hit. He tried to push himself backwards, away from the angry man that moved toward him with his hands clenched. The father continued to advance on him.

"Get going honey, I'll take care of this."

"Bill! Just leave him alone. Let's go," the woman said.

Davy tried to explain, but he stuttered and fumbled his words.

The father stopped, but his hands remained balled into fists. His eyes locked on Davy, but he slowly turned and joined his family.

"He could be some sort of pervert, Ryan. That's why you have to stay with us." He had grabbed his wife's and Ryan's hands and had pulled them down the trail.

"He's a retard," the man had said. "What's wrong with you, Ryan? You stay away from those people!"

Davy was backpedaling the whole time and only gibberish came out of his mouth. He wasn't able to mutter a word. He felt a small wave of relief when the man turned away, but he still couldn't get his thoughts working. He wanted to cry. As the family moved off down the trail, Davy saw Ryan turn back and smile one more time. Davy forced a smile back. When they hiked out of sight, Davy rolled over and got back to his feet. He used his hands to brush the dirt and leaves off the seat of his pants, then he noticed the dark wet spot on the crotch of his pants. He had wet himself. He stared at the blotch in horror. I'm grown up now; I'm not supposed to wet myself, he thought. He felt his face go hot and he looked quickly behind him. He was grateful that no one saw. He moved off the path and hid behind a tree where he sat holding back tears until his pants dried enough to go back on the trail. He made it home just before dark.

Davy wiped his face with his hands. The memory of that day still made him a little shaky. Davy thought the angry man reminded him of a man from his past, one that stuck him in closets and hit him. Davy looked around his small apartment half expecting to see that man even though he had been gone for many years. Davy exhaled, shook his head and put on his biggest smile. He put down the maps and went about his routine of getting ready to go to work. He knew that was the best way to forget his past.

***

Davy looked around his small second floor apartment to make sure he turned off all the lights. He lived several blocks from the supermarket but it was only one bus stop for him to get to work. It was only one bedroom with a small living room and kitchen, but he tried to make it look nice. He bought furniture from Goodwill and Salvation Army to fill it. Davy had an old television. In the kitchen sat an old off-white refrigerator spotted with rust, an electric stove, old and clean, and a sink. He did his dishes all the time so the roaches wouldn't come in. He hated those nasty bugs. Notes, schedules, and reminders hung in neat rows down the front of his refrigerator. Davy looked at the notes and read each one carefully. As he finished one, he checked to see if he had done what it said. The notes were reminders to check the stove, set his alarm, check to make sure he had his keys, bus fare, and almost every other important task he had to remember. Davy was very careful about reading the notes every morning and every afternoon. It was the key to him being able to live alone. List complete, Davy locked up and walked to the bus stop. Time to go to work.

***

Davy stepped out of the bathroom back into the stockroom. He pushed slowly through the double doors, careful not to hit any customers. He looked down the aisle all the way to the plate glass window in the front. He laughed at the store name; it was painted backwards on the front glass. He saw it every day but it was always funny to him. Davy passed by one of the other boys that worked there.

He was pricing cans and putting them on the shelves. Sometimes Mr. Harrington allowed him to price goods with the push stamp. Mostly he carted boxes, mopped floors, and helped people out with their groceries. He had been working there for over two years and he loved it. He loved his life.

Davy brushed his hand through his thick black hair that fell right back in place. When he did this, it reminded him, like his friends at the home, he was special, though it wasn't the special he wanted. He didn't feel sorry for himself. He was used to the stares he received from the shoppers. He just smiled and went about his tasks.

Davy didn't know if it was his looks or his smile, but he noticed early on that he had a special talent. He seemed to be able to calm children with a look and he saw children all day long. Mothers filled the store, hurrying to do their shopping, racing up and down aisles looking for the right items, and a lot of the time they were pulling unhappy children along. Others just strolled through the store; a child riding in a shopping cart.

When children saw him, they would stare and Davy would always smile his biggest smile. Sometimes they returned his smile, sometimes not. He wished he could go over and tickle them to make them happy, but knew that wasn't allowed. One day, he saw a little boy sitting in the front of the shopping cart. He was about five and was dressed in blue overalls. Davy moved across the aisle so the boy could see him. When the boy looked up at Davy, Davy smiled and thought about tickling the boy's ribs. The child's smile broadened and he began to laugh. Ever since then, Davy would send tickles to all the children. Some would break out in laughter and some even put their arms out. Davy loved children.

As Davy worked, he watched for chances make children smile. Once, Davy saw one mother fretting and exasperated with shopping, about to spank her child for reaching for candy. Davy hurried toward her and the little girl hoping to stop the spanking.

"Let me help you," he said.

Davy hoped to stop the punishment by settling the child with a tickle. This time he was too late and he stood helplessly by as the mother administered two slaps to the little girl's backside. Davy felt the child's pain, both emotional and physical, as he always did when he was close. But Davy didn't let his disappointment or sadness show, even when his pain felt as great as the child's. When the mother returned to her task, Davy searched out the child's eyes and projected love and comfort into them. The little girl stopped crying and just stared through tear filled eyes. Davy then sent a tickle and she smiled back.

Davy had tried several times in the past to project into parents, too, but it never worked. They never maintained eye contact long enough. They acted scared of him.

Davy went back to sweeping aisle three and then he would do four. He carefully swept under the edges to get everything. After aisle four, Davy went into the back to eat his lunch. He heard his boss, Mr. Harrington, page him over the loudspeaker. Davy put away the half of his sandwich he hadn't finished and went to the office. Mr. Harrington stood by his desk and in his chair sat a little girl, crying.

"Davy. Thanks for coming. I've seen how you are with kids. Can you help? I can't get her to quit crying. She's lost," Mr. Harrington said.

"Yes, sir," Davy replied. "Hi there. What's your name?"

The little girl looked up for just a moment, then back down ,but she lifted her head again. Davy looked right at her eyes and put on a big smile. He imagined a light tickle flowing from his head, out of his eyes, into hers, and ending in her belly. The little girl smiled.

"Good job, Davy," Mr. Harrington said. "Can you get her name please?"

He turned and grabbed his mike. "There is a missing child in the manager's office. Please, if you are missing a child come to the manager's office."

Davy looked at the little girl and gave her a warm comforting feeling. "My name is Davy. What's yours?"

"I'm Jenny," she said.

"Well, hi, Jenny. Mr. Harrington is a nice man. He'll find your mom."

"I was supposed to wait with the cart but I went to look at the candy."

"I like candy, too," Davy said.

There was a knock at the door and Mr. Harrington slipped out. He was gone for just a second and came back in with a woman. Davy noticed she was very pale and her eyes wide and wet like she'd been crying. She raced past Davy and scooped up the girl.

"Jenny, Jenny! I'm sorry. Mommy's sorry," she cried to the little girl.

The little girl started crying again.

"I'm sorry, too, mommy."

The two left the office.

"Thank you, Davy. You really have a way with the little guys. You can be my child specialist," Mr. Harrington said.

"Yes, sir, Mr. Harrington, I can tickle children," Davy said with his smile covering his face.

He saw Mr. Harrington's smile disappear.

"Davy, you can never touch a child in the store. You understand?"

"Yes, Mr. Harrington." Now Davy felt a little scared by the look on Mr. Harrington's face.

"I never touch them Mr. Harrington. I do it by looking at them and sending one to them."

Mr. Harrington's smile didn't reappear and now Davy saw his eyebrows rise up. Davy thought maybe he had said something wrong.

"As long as you never touch them."

Davy returned to the lunch room feeling good that he could help and that Mr. Harrington thought of him as his child specialist. He finished eating before returning to sweeping.

***

Tuesday after work Davy went to the park. Mr. Harrington always let him take a loaf of out of date bread to feed the pigeons. He strolled along the stone trail and found a place on a bench by a small lake. He picked off a small chunk and tossed it out into the grass. He smiled as three pigeons raced to grab it. He liked the way their feathers looked like rainbows when they moved. Davy looked across the way and saw three women on a bench talking while their little children chased each other by the swings. The children paused when they saw the commotion of the birds fighting for the bread. When Davy saw them, he stood. He walked toward them to give them some slices to also feed the birds. Before he got too close, the mothers called their children to them. Their looks made Davy feel bad. He went back to the bench, but he wasn't as happy anymore. He looked back at the women with their children leaving the park. He wondered why they were so afraid of him. After all, he was just a dumb old stock boy. That thought made him smile. That's what his friend, Roberta, at the Independent Living Class, called him.

Davy remembered when he first saw Roberta. He was about fourteen. Roberta came to Destiny House when she was eight. The first time Davy saw her, she just stared and didn't smile. Now that they were friends, she smiled more and he found that other than her memory, she was pretty smart about things. She always tried to explain to Davy new things she learned. He smiled thinking about it. He knew when she began explaining things he would just nod his head. He tried once to tell her he already knew the things she said, but that made her mad and she refused to speak to him the rest of the evening. Even though they argued sometimes, they liked to joke around and tease each other. She would call him a dumb old stock boy and he would call her a silly girl. Roberta had a problem with remembering things. Sometimes she couldn't remember things minutes after she was told.

Davy thought she liked him and he knew he liked her. Even though he doubted she could ever get away from the house on her own, he thought maybe someday they could get married and then he could have a baby of his own to hold and play with all the time.

On Thursday, Davy had to stack boxes from a delivery in the back and then cart out cases of paper goods to the aisle for the other men to mark and put on the shelves. Out of the corner of his eye, Davy saw a small boy riding in his mother's shopping cart. Davy looked at the boy. He felt a chill and something else, something cold and heavy. It came from both the boy's arm and inside. Davy had felt something like it before, sometimes sharp, sometimes dull. Most of the time, he knew it came from being sick like with a cold, but the dull pain, the dark stuff he knew was different. It was like the pain he felt when he had been spanked as a child. When the boy looked at Davy, Davy knew the pain came from the mother.

Davy left his box in the aisle and went to the office.

"Mr. Harrington," Davy said. "Come quick. There's a hurt child."

Mr. Harrington jumped up and followed Davy.

Davy called over his shoulder. "I think it's his mother hurting him."

Davy almost slid around a corner and pointed.

All Mr. Harrington saw was a mother with a sad looking child in the cart and nothing more.

"Sorry ma'am, we're looking for someone else."

Mr. Harrington took him back to the office.

 "Davy! What were you talking about?"

"It's the child, Mr. Harington. Remember how you said I had a way with children. I could feel the boy was hurt and I think his mother is hurting him."

Mr. Harrington looked at Davy's worried face. Mr. Harrington took a deep breath. He really liked the kid. He had to find a way to explain it better to him.

"If you see anybody hurting a child, I mean see it not feel it, you come straight to me and I'll handle it. Understood? We can't accuse them just because you think so. That wouldn't be good. "

"But Mr. Harrington, the boy, his arm is hurt."

"I saw that Davy, but what does that mean? He's a little boy and little boys are always getting hurt."

"His mother did it." Davy was determined.

"How do you know that? Did you see her? Are you positive it was her?"

Davy thought for a moment. Maybe it wasn't the mother, maybe the father. No, the mother caused it, the darkness inside told him, though Davy didn't know how to explain it to Mr. Harrington.

"I'm pretty sure, Mr. Harrington."

Mr. Harrington looked at Davy. What could he say? The boy meant well but he just didn't understand. It might be partly his fault for telling Davy that he was his child specialist. He did have a way with children though. He had seen it with his own eyes.

"I'll tell you what I'll do, Davy. I'll watch her on the store cameras and see if I can catch her, but you have to stay away from her and the boy, okay?"

"Yes, sir," said Davy, proud that he had been able to do something.

Mr. Harrington watched him leave and then went back to his paperwork.

Davy checked his watch. It was time to go and catch the bus to the Destiny Center for his Independent Living Class. As he left the store he imagined his friends in the class.

***

Davy's friends lived at Destiny House. He was the only one that had graduated. He knew they would swamp him with questions. They always wanted to know what it was like to live alone. He could imagine Bobby asking if he saw burglars, his eyes wide and his hands on his cheeks. Little Mary would just follow him around without talking. Betty would ignore him 'cause she was jealous. Betty was mean. Harold would ask about his job and how much money he made. He would ask Davy if he could see some money. He shook his head slowly, sad, because he knew a lot of them would never get out like him. Then he smiled because he would get to see Roberta. Davy liked being independent.

THREE

The ulasiga contracted its gelled form when it felt the vibrations. It quickly focused on the source above. It felt the steady rhythmic tremors that indicated something living, instead of the natural shaking of landslides, falling trees, even the minute impact of pine cones. When it found a pattern, every cell inside the being went on alert. It noted the direction and speed. Assured it was a living thing, the ulasiga pushed its mental waves. It used every cell, each almost independent of the whole, first to unlock the thought patterns and determine what drove its prey. Then it would generate the necessary signals to lure the victim. If successful, it could draw its prey to the darkness.

The ulasiga began the slow journey from its lair deep below. It extended itself through the dark, sliding over rock, weaving through cracks toward the minute vibration that had awakened it. It paused to judge the distance to the prey. The source moved closer. Whatever had been moving outside the cave, had come close enough, perhaps stopping to rest in the shade provided by the cave. The ulasiga could feel the heartbeat through the rock. It focused on the intruder, sending out signals to relax the potential meal. It integrated the brain waves of the victim with its own, taking over control and easing it down, using what could be termed mental morphine. It could sense the victim's heart beat slowing, body functions decreasing, and then sleep.

The predator continued the journey toward the now comatose body. It thinned its jellied body to ease through the gaps, sometimes making itself only a few cells thick. It stretched out as far as it dared, keeping the major portion of its body squeezed in the cracks it had traveled through. Even if the victim remained alert, it wouldn't feel the presence of the monster. The ulasiga worked its way around inside the rock to the top of a cave it had known so well, serving as a dining area for hundreds of years. Through a small crack in the roof it dropped a thin line of cells from the ceiling. It slowly stretched out feeling for any of the burning light until it made contact. A charge of feelings swept down its length, through every cell of its being. The last visions seen by the victim appeared in the creature's mind like a movie. The ulasiga stilled itself, captivated by the scenes unfolding before it as seen through the eyes of its future meal. The ulasiga watched green grass part and dirt underfoot pass, as its prey's mind replayed the last few moments of its life. The ulasiga watched as the scene shifted to a nose sniffing the ground. The show ended as the short lived memory of the rodent faded. No longer able to interpret the images, the predator blocked the brain waves that kept the creature breathing. Respiration stopped and death followed as quiet and uneventful as dawn. The ulasiga began the task of dissolving the meal. Its caustic juices melted hair, bone, and sinew. It turned the mouse into soup and transferred it along its length, consuming some, depositing the rest in its lair.

Another vibration alerted the ulasiga to the advance of another creature, familiar to the ulasiga from long ago; two feet, heavy, man. Once before, this ulasiga had encountered man. Then that food source had disappeared. It recalled it could manipulate the brain waves as easily as the other animals. In addition to size, the length and clarity of man's memory made him special. The imagery would last for hours and hours. Unfortunately for the ulasiga, the few men it had caught centuries ago died too quickly and the show had been cut short. It knew next time it encountered man, it would allow him to live at the edge of death, letting the images run their full course. Man made the perfect meal, dinner and a show, and both would last for a long time.

FOUR

A few weeks after his encounter with the angry man, Davy began to think about going hiking again. He was angry with himself for getting so scared. He looked into the mirror and asked himself, "Are you a man or a baby?"

Davy grabbed his trail map, determined to go and take another hike. The leaves had started to turn color but there was still plenty of daylight to hike. He looked at the large map he had taken from the ranger station that showed all the trails. He had colored all the ones he had been on before, but one trail he had never followed, the longest and the hardest trial on the map. That wasn't the reason Davy had never taken the trail. He opened his crayon box and began to look for the color he needed to make his index card. He found it in the back row, in the corner, sharp as the day it was bought. Davy didn't like the color. It was black; black as a moonless night; dark as a closet, fearful as a monster. But Davy told himself to not be afraid. He was a man now and men were not scared of the night. Besides, it was just a hike up a trail. Wasn't he Davy Crockett; King of the Wild Frontier? He would prove he wasn't a scaredy baby.

He took the number five bus to the terminal and then took the number ten out of town to the Sascone Peak Trailhead parking lot. Davy wasn't surprised that the parking lot was almost empty because he had taken the first bus of the day and the sun still sat behind the mountains. He checked his backpack one more time; water, granola bars, first aid kit, whistle, and flashlight, just as he'd been taught. He strapped it on and walked to where the trail entered the woods. He pulled out the index card from his shirt pocket. The black circle on the white background sent a chill into Davy and he stared at it for a long time. It looked like the rim to a deep well; a cold, dark well. The damp walls would be slippery and once inside there'd be no escape. A shiver ran up his back and made his scalp tickle. He reached up and mussed his own hair to make the weird feeling disappear. He replaced his cap and put the card back in his pocket.

He looked for the first tree with a black splash of paint and saw it less than ten feet up the trail. He began his hike, first up the steep climbing trail and then at a slight incline as it wound its way around the mountain.

After a while, Davy stopped and sat on a recently fallen tree. He ran his hand up and down the smooth bark coating the downfall. He wished he knew what kind it was. He tried to learn the different kinds of trees using his encyclopedia at home but his memory wasn't good enough.

Instead, he pulled a leaf off one of the branches and slipped it in his pack. He glanced up and down the trail looking for the black splotches on the trees that marked his route. When he saw them, a tingle of fear ran through him again. He remembered Snow White, or was it Cinderella? One of them had been lost and wandered around the forest, a dark and scary forest. Davy looked around him and could see how frightening this forest could be in the dark. He had gone farther than he had ever hiked before. He looked at his watch to see the time. He knew when both hands came together at the top, it would be time to go home.

He looked around again. It seemed strange that trees could grow out of the sides of a mountain. He listened for squirrels running through the underbrush and heard nothing. He could barely see the sky above because the mountains and trees hid most of it. He took a deep breath and let it out slowly. Yep, he thought, I'm a man.

A soft cry coming from behind him drew his attention. He sat stiffly upright and turned his head toward the sound, but it had stopped. Davy waited breathlessly, still as a statue. It sounded like a child crying or calling tearfully for help. He turned and looked into the forest behind him trying to see who made the sound. He heard the cry again from behind the wall of trees. This time he was ready for it and sure enough, it sounded like a cry of a child; one who had been at it a while, ragged and short. It stopped almost as soon as it began. He looked up and down the trail looking for any other hikers, someone to help him, but there wasn't a single person in sight. He realized he hadn't seen anyone all day. As far as he knew, he might be the only one on this trail today. The cry came again. This time it came from farther away. It scared him to think that a lost child may be walking the wrong way, deeper into the woods. He knew he had to go look.

"Wait! I'm coming! Over here!" he shouted in the direction of the sound. With shaky legs he left the trail, moving toward where he had heard it last. It came again and Davy hurried in that direction hoping to get there before the child moved deeper into the forest or he lost sight of the fallen tree. When he had gone as far as he dared, he stopped and waited. He knew another cry would come soon. It did and now it came from closer than before, although up the hillside, and again Davy hurried toward it. The next time he stopped, he shouted again and looked for the child. When the noise sound again, it had moved farther away. Davy had been walking fast toward it but didn't seem to gain any ground. He tore his pants on a branch hidden in a clump of bushes. He stopped and untangled himself, then continued up the side of the mountain. He stopped and yelled for the child again. This time, when the cry came, he jumped. The sound came from right above him. He looked up and saw a bird sitting on a branch over his head. He stood for what seemed an eternity and then the bird ruffled its feathers and let out another squawk that sounded like that of a small child. Davy just stood there, mouth agape. He watched the bird for some time, listening again and again to the sound it made until it flew away. Davy pounded his forehead for being so easily fooled. He stood there for a moment, angry at himself. Once he calmed down, he let his mind probe the area in case it hadn't been the bird or perhaps it had been both. He didn't feel any children around, happy or sad. Davy looked back the way he came then checked his watch. He still had one or two go rounds left before both hands would come together. He turned toward where he thought the trail ran and began walking in that direction.

After a few minutes of steady hiking, Davy began to worry. He should have reached it by now. He looked through the trees trying to spot the dirt path. Trees, leaves, and branches filled the forest, but there was no sign of the trail. He started out again, a little slower, now looking at all the trees, looking for a black splash. Davy ran out of trees as he came up against the rocky side of the mountain. He knew then, he had missed the trail. He looked behind him and saw the whole valley below. Davy realized he had never been so high. His fear momentarily forgotten, he stared at the view. He could see the line of mountains that edged along the city laid out below, miles away. He tried to spot the supermarket and the group home. He knew somewhere behind the trees and hills sat the parking lot that marked the trailhead. At first, he wanted to walk straight down the hill toward the city, but he remembered what he had been taught about moving around in the woods when lost. Instead, he would retrace his steps. Davy heard a rumble up and behind him, above the mountain peak. What sky he could see had gone black with rain clouds. He felt the first big drop hit him in the head, heavy and very cold. He had to stop himself from running. He put his hands on his temples and closed his eyes. It was one of the ways he had taught himself to calm down. It's only rain, he told himself, and rain will stop. He began searching for a boulder or some kind of cutout he could hide under. He didn't want to stand in the freezing rain. He made his way along the rocks. He squeezed into one hole, but the rain still found him. He pulled himself back out and continued along the wall of the mountain. The rain came harder and with it a brilliant flash of lightning. Davy put his back up against a huge rock. Here, most of the rain missed him, but another bolt passed overhead with a loud explosion of thunder. Davy felt, more than saw, the small opening to the cave. Something made him step around the large boulder and look behind it. He saw an entrance. He moved to the mouth of the dark hole, pulled off his pack, and took out his flashlight. Davy shined it inside.

The ulasiga began its journey now. This vibration felt big and stumbling. The ulasiga sent an invitation. It moved directly for the opening in the cave. The ulasiga could also feel the pounding of rain on rock. Its potential meal walked on the surface where light shone and the creature couldn't go. Halfway to the opening, the ulasiga's prey paused. The movement had stopped, just shy of the cave.

At first, Davy only saw rock walls and a dirt floor. The resemblance to a closet became almost overwhelming until the next bolt of lightning split the sky and a cold fat drop of rain penetrated Davy's shirt. Davy bent down and entered the cave. Sweeping his light around the area, he saw several small clay pots, most broken. Two mounds that looked like blankets sat up against one rock wall. When Davy touched them with his toe, they fell to dust. Indians! The roar of thunder, so close it felt like it came from inside the cave, made Davy cringe. Davy moved as close to the entrance as he could without getting wet and sat down. He didn't want to waste his batteries so he turned off his flashlight and stared at the dull light coming through the opening. It looked small and dark, very scary. He occasionally checked behind him, looking for anything sneaking up to grab him.

He sat there and watched as the rain poured down. When the lightning split the sky, he pulled up tight against the wall of rock. Davy sat in a state of panic as all his mistakes came to him in flashes. The cry he remembered now sounded more like a mocking laugh; the kind of laugh that followed him around the school when the kids teased him. He pounded his forehead as he thought of the lost trail. The trees stood everywhere and they no longer looked friendly. Here in the cave, he stayed safe from the rain and lightning, but no matter what he tried to tell himself, it was a closet, the same as all the others he had been locked in when he was a child. At least in here, the door stayed open. Davy remembered the last time he had been this scared. He had wet himself then. He reached down and felt his crotch. It was still dry. That brought a bit of relief. Davy scrounged around inside his backpack feeling for the flashlight again. Maybe he could find a corner he could pee in, just in case.

While the ulasiga waited, it focused its attention on the intended meal. Instead of judging size and movement, it tried to pick up thought patterns. This animal above projected its own waves deeper into the cave than any previous prey. The ulasiga couldn't interpret the thought patterns, even though it could certainly feel them. It eased off on the reception of the prey and continued to get closer.

Now, only yards away, the ulasiga stopped again and concentrated more on the brain waves coming from above. The waves felt strong and resembled man, yet different, less complex. The patterns flowed fast and jagged, except for the ones that controlled the heart and lungs. The intended victim remained out of range even if it could reach out and shut down the signals. What good was a comatose victim it couldn't reach? It began the task of putting the signals together, learning them, understanding them, so perhaps it could use them to lure the meal closer.

The ulasiga began to latch onto and decipher the brain patterns from this meal that hovered just out of range. In the past it had perceived panic in some of its victims, although most died quietly, unafraid and not even knowing they were being lead to slaughter. This one reverberated fear and the ulasiga could feel the unease. It could also feel change in the intensity as this creature, a man, flipped through several levels of alarm. The ulasiga had to work hard at keeping up with the jagged thoughts and still the man sat out of range. Would it venture deeper? The thoughts that controlled movement were being held in check, in fact ordered to stop. It could feel the terror the man had of the dark. Could the ulasiga lay a wave over it and calm the agitated man? Could it substitute another wave for the one afraid of the dark? It searched for signals it could use and mimic. It searched for anything longer in wavelength, something that calmed the man. It found several. One it found was tied to a single thought, Davy, which the ulasiga determined to be what the man called itself. The ulasiga tried it. There was some change that smoothed the patterns, but not enough. It continued to search. Another appeared to be stronger. It didn't understand the meaning, but that wasn't necessary. It located a feeling, a gentle wave, relief from the panic. The ulasiga studied the pattern for just a moment and then began knitting its own between the shorter jagged ones. It began slowly and deliberately so it wouldn't confuse the man Davy. It sent the signals out and then paused to receive the effect.

FIVE

Davy felt the change instantly, although it felt different from anything he had ever experienced. He had always sent happy feelings to the children in the store. Not all of them, just the ones that seemed to need it, the children hurt or sad. The images and feelings came softly from them, but what he felt now was strong, forced in. He knew somewhere underneath he was really scared, but he was feeling better. It felt like what he tied to project to the children. He tried to feel out the source as he did in the store. The storm, the dark, being lost, everything suddenly was okay. He mentally tried to grab the incoming thought like a kid trying to grasp a trout in a stream. It managed to slip away whenever he thought he had it isolated. It remained tied too closely to his own thoughts to separate and still he knew it came from outside. It didn't worry him; in fact it delighted him to think someone else may be nearby. He instinctively looked around trying to locate the source, anxious to see the person responsible, but the cave looked empty. Maybe they were outside in the forest, Davy thought. Then he remembered the rain and lightning outside. Whoever it was had to be somewhere in this cave. He moved toward the back, his fear of the dark forgotten.

Davy took his flashlight and used it to sweep the walls with the light, looking for hidden corners or openings. He saw a smaller hole near the back, big enough to wiggle through, certainly enough for a child. Maybe a lost child had come in here and crawled through. Davy got down on his hands and knees and peered in the mouth of the hole. He couldn't see anything in the total darkness of the other room. Using his flashlight, he swept the room. Suddenly, he felt a tearing pain behind his eyes. He dropped the light and grabbed both sides of his head, squeezing hard to stop the stabbing he felt in his head.

"Owowowow," he cried.

It felt like a long wooden sliver being shoved into his brain from his ear. Finally the pain went away and he sat up slowly rubbing his temples. The mysterious visitor had left his head. It must be one of those mergrain, magraine, something headaches. He picked up the light and shone it into the hole again. He could see the smaller room on the other side of the opening. It could hold him, but not much more. On the far side, a small wet spot steamed as if hot water leaked into the cave.

"Hello," he shouted.

The ulasiga had fled back into the mountain at the flash of light. The sudden onslaught had caught it by surprise. The burn, the loss of some of its body, hurt. Nothing in its experience could account for what had happened. Like a wounded animal, it held still, waiting, wondering.

It could still feel the vibrations of 'the' Davy moving about in the outer chamber. Slowly, it began probing back toward him, this time more carefully. A meal was still a meal and man was quite a prize.

Davy turned away from the small hole and sat back on the ground. He had thought he had heard crying and had gone too deep into the woods only to find a bird apparently teasing him. Now he sat in this tiny cave. He had felt a connection in his mind and found nobody around. What if it had been a child and it had crawled inside the cave? Maybe the bird had been mocking what it heard. It was possible wasn't it; the bird leading him to a lost child, much like Lassie leading Timmy? What if the little kid had found the cave and had continued deeper, where he couldn't see? He looked outside and saw that the rain had slacked off and the lightning stopped, although he could still hear far away rumblings of thunder. He shined his light on his watch and saw the one long hand had moved half way around to leaving time and he still didn't know how to find the trail. He knew he should leave right away.

He put the flashlight back into his pack and began crawling toward the opening. Just before he ducked to squeeze out, he paused. He worried that he might be leaving a scared child. He just couldn't do that. He remembered the comforting feeling and didn't want to abandon the child that had sent it. He turned and crawled back to the little opening in the back of the cave. He stuck his head in and then began to concentrate, sending out his own comforting thoughts.

The ulasiga stopped short as it picked up the wave traveling down a long tunnel. It came from the Davy and it moved closer. The ulasiga had very little knowledge of the Davy to draw on so it hesitated, capturing the waves and digesting them, waiting to see what would follow. It had felt the Davy moving away toward the opening where the ulasiga knew it couldn't go. It couldn't do anything about it, but now the Davy returned. The ulasiga felt it calling. It was too big of a meal to let go so easily and yet it appeared dangerous.

The ulasiga started sending out small signals like it had the first time to see what would happen. It wanted the Davy mostly for the huge food supply, but it also wanted the memory. In hundreds of years, surrounded by nothing but rock and reliving the few hazy memories of rodents and small animals, the ulasiga desired more.

SIX

Again, Davy felt something, a feeling, just not like what he felt coming from children. But what else could it be, he wondered. He had never been able to get anything from adults. From children, he always received the feelings, feelings of happiness, sadness, joy, and fear. He squeezed his eyes shut and focused on what he was feeling. It was almost the same as what he sent. It felt like being mimicked. Anger came first as he remembered the teasing growing up but then what he felt changed. Davy got excited when he thought he might find someone who would understand him and the things he could do. Noon passed without so much as another thought. Davy tried to wiggle through the small opening, into the darker inner chamber. He had lost his fear in his excitement. He almost got stuck, but even that didn't worry him as the feelings of comfort and relief continued to flow in. He backed out of the small entrance and the feelings weakened. He hurried to enlarge the hole with his hands. He pulled away loose rock. He dug at the floor with his hands like a dog searching for a bone. When he had removed some of the loose debris, he stuck his head back in and pushed out a stronger touch toward the back of the inner chamber, one that oozed with comfort.

The ulasiga felt it all. When it received the surge of new waves, it imitated them also. It felt the Davy working his way closer. If he could entice the Davy into the darker small chamber, then he may be far enough away from the light for the ulasiga to reach. Then it would induce the Davy's body into a coma-like state. The ulasiga could consume him over the next several weeks, transferring much to its underground chamber. The ulasiga continued the flow of waves while monitoring the progress of the Davy through the vibration in the rock. The ulasiga wasn't willing to expose itself to the opening after the recent burn it received. It lay there almost pulsing with anticipation, continuing to try to draw him closer, powering up the signals. The ulasiga understood that if it stopped the body functions at this distance, then it would be unable to absorb the memories and the ulasiga desired the memories now, even more than the meal.

At last Davy wiggled enough to squeeze through the opening. He felt his way into the room. He remembered it as small and tried to find the other side with his hands. He reached for his flashlight and remembered he had left it and his bag in the other chamber in his excitement to get in. He looked back for the opening and found that all he could see was a gray spot among the blackness to mark the entrance. He turned back and waved his hands around to see if he could touch the person sending the signals.

"Is there someone in here?" he asked.

He waited. His labored breathing masked any other sound. As he turned to go back out to get his pack something once again pulled at him. He turned again toward the blackness.

"Who's there?" he called. He waved his hands around in front of him.

"Don't worry, I won't hurt you," he said. All he found was the ceiling. Davy inched his way forward. The room remained black. His eyes didn't adjust as he hoped they might. He continued to call out.

"Don't be afraid," he said. The sound died like yelling into his pillow. But whoever was back there wasn't afraid. Davy could feel that. He turned and looked back the way he had come. Davy began to get a little scared. It felt too much like the closet. He turned once more toward the feeling that was and wasn't like that from a child. Then that urge, the call, got a little bit stronger, so he continued his blind travel toward the back of the cave. Using his hands to protect him, Davy felt the tunnel change direction and the impossible darkness became even darker. He sat for a moment to let his eyes adjust. Like when he woke at night in his apartment. If he waited, his darkened room always got lighter. This inky blackness was different. Davy pulled his hand toward his face and squinted, straining to see. Nothing. At this point Davy decided to turn and retreat. He couldn't imagine anyone back in this darkness and he had been fooled once today. As soon as he faced the direction toward the other entrance, a wave of sleepiness rolled over him. He sat down to rest for a moment, hung his head and closed his eyes. That it wasn't any darker with his eyes closed than opened crossed his mind just before sleep captured him.

The ulasiga rested, too. It had burned up precious energy working the thought patterns and reacting to the constant change in feeling. It kept the man's brainwaves at the level required to maintain life.

Rested, the ulasiga moved closer for better control. It began the process of shutting down the Davy.

It maintained the pace of the lungs and heart just enough to ensure the meal didn't die. Slowly, still wary from the fright and pain of its first attempt, the ulasiga moved closer. Strand by strand, cell by cell, it ventured tentatively forward. It moved a significant portion of its boneless body into the inner chamber. It could feel the heat coming off the sleeping Davy from several feet away. It could time the steady in and out of his breathing from the vibration off the floor of the cave. Slowly, the ulasiga moved in. It started picking up touches of waves, strange patterns that switched quickly and then would stop. It could feel the orbs in the Davy's head move about quickly from side to side and then up and down whenever these signals began. It paused, wondering if the Davy were indeed awake.

Davy just wanted to close his eyes for just a second. When he did, he found himself back in the supermarket mopping up a broken jar of jelly. Only this supermarket looked much bigger and brighter. Instead of it coming up easily, the jelly smeared into a big splotch on the floor. The purple circle just kept getting larger and Davy thought he could feel Mr. Harrington coming, only it wasn't Mr. Harrington, it was the mean man on the trail. He heard a child crying over on the next aisle. He dropped his mop and ran around to the other side to find the source of the wailing. A bird pecked at the floor for a second then it looked right at him. It squawked its mocking call, then its face turned into the face of the man on the trail.

"Retard, retard," he said.

The man ruffled his feathers and flapped his wings, flying to the next aisle over. Davy followed it there. Again the aisle appeared empty except for the strange birdman that opened his beak and let out another string of insults.

"Dummy, dummy, dummy," it squawked.

Davy turned to go back to his mopping. When he rounded the corner, the store disappeared and he found himself standing in the woods. He called out for help and got no answer. He turned to go back the way he had come and found himself surrounded by walls, not trees.

When he turned back, he stood in his living room and the cry came from within his closet. He walked slowly to the closed door and listened. Sure enough, he heard a small child whimpering inside. He tried the door but it wouldn't open. Backing up a few steps, he tried to send thoughts of comfort through the door and realized nothing came out. Something had changed inside and his mind would not release the thoughts. He tried the door again and this time it came open in his grasp. It looked empty, but he could only see as far as the light went and that wasn't all the way to the back. From deep inside he heard the sniffling child. Without another thought, Davy rushed in, crossing from light to dark, to find the child. He called out as he went. The child's cries seemed to get no closer or farther away. Davy turned to see how far inside the closet he had wandered and saw the door hundreds of feet back, swinging shut. He wanted to run toward it, catch it before it closed all the way, but his legs suddenly felt heavy and tired. He couldn't get them to move. When it shut, everything went black.

The ulasiga stopped its manipulations when it felt the legs of the Davy start kicking. It knew that one strike could separate some of its body, in effect, killing a portion of it. It sent out new commands and slowed the breathing more until all external movement ceased. Slowly it approached the Davy, careful not to touch him. It didn't want to kill just yet. When it hovered close enough, the waves of memories began to download. The most recent memories came first and the creature remained motionless as it watched the show. It understood little of what it saw, but learned that this man lived outside in the world of light. It almost broke the connection and retreated into its lair when it encountered the first memory of a bright sunny day. Then came the children. The ulasiga hung just above the Davy watching a parade of smaller versions of man. It felt, rather than saw, the attraction they had to this larger one. It noticed the brainwaves generated from the man as the images appeared matched the ones the ulasiga used to calm him earlier. It saw the little men smile. It found their names; children, babies, kids. The ulasiga watched, pondered, learned.

After a while, the ulasiga broke the connection and retreated back into familiar dark territory. It washed the memories up and down its length. It sent them through each cell and each cell in turn sent back signals. It had much to learn and the possibilities were astounding if the right trigger could be found. The ulasiga eased the block and allowed the Davy to breathe normally. It didn't want this one dead. This one was special. This one could supply the ulasiga with food for a long, long, time. It went back to the Davy and reconnected with his mind. The ulasiga began searching for the information it needed.

SEVEN

Roberta hung up the phone. Where was that butthead now, she wondered? He's probably at the playground feeding the birds or at the store being a dumb old stock boy. She turned and waddled down the hallway, crossing through the entertainment room where several of her fellow housemates watched TV or played board games. She lifted her chubby hand in a half hearted greeting and continued back to her room. She had some studying to do if she ever wanted to get out of this house. She had been writing down her grocery list; homework from the Independent Living Classes, and got stuck on a word. She couldn't remember what they called the long thin noodles. One of the others in the house probably knew, but she was too embarrassed to ask. They would laugh and tease her. Besides, it gave her a reason to call Davy. Talking to him made her feel better even if they mostly called each other names. It was just in fun and she knew it.

She was disappointed when he hadn't been there. Now she would have to finish on her own. I'll call again later, when it gets dark, she thought. He's always home before dark.

She reached out and grabbed the doorknob to her room and found it locked. She jiggled it again and it still wouldn't open.

"Wrong room, doofus," said Betty from down the hall.

Roberta looked up and sure enough a number five hung from the nail and her door had a number seven. She could feel herself turning red. She quickly covered her embarrassment with a lie.

"I was looking for Jennifer, stupid," she said without turning.

"I bet you were," said Betty. "Jennifer's room is number three." Betty held up three fat fingers for Roberta to see.

Roberta just stood there, fuming, as Betty squeezed by.

Roberta moved down to her room and went in, closing the door behind her. She sat at her desk and began pounding on her head.

"Stupid, stupid, stupid."

She looked down at her unfinished list and her mind returned to the problem that had sent her from her room in the first place, her encounter with Betty already fading.

Roberta looked into the mirror over her desk. She silently pleaded with her image to remember that Betty picked on her again. She grabbed her pencil and wrote, "Betty is a mean dope." She looked around her desk at the sheets of paper with her handwriting. She closed her eyes. She thought about living away from this place, living in her own home. She remembered 911 for emergencies. She remembered the address to this place. She could remember to turn off the lights and check the stove to be sure it was off. She knew the TV room was down the hall, the kitchen on the left, the front and back door, the telephone, and all the light switches. Just because she couldn't remember little things was no reason to make her stay here with what's her name. She opened her eyes and read the paper in front of her. Betty, that's the one. Why did she have to live here with Betty? She threw her pencil. The minute she let go, she regretted it. She knew it would hit the wall, maybe leaving a mark. That wouldn't be good. She could get in trouble and lose privileges. Betty would laugh. In an instant, she deflected its flight with a thought and it tumbled harmlessly to the floor. Roberta scratched her head and stared at the pencil lying on the carpet. She knew that she had stopped it from hitting the wall just by wanting it, something about looking at it, but she was already forgetting how.

She stood up and walked across the room to retrieve the pencil and when she did, she found herself face to face with her image, glaring back from the mirror hung on the back of the door to her room. She quickly looked away. She didn't want to see her face; the puffy cheeks and extra chin, or her eyes; big, round, and slightly tilted, the ones that made people look the other way. She didn't want to see her short straight black hair. She scanned down her body instead. She put her hands on her hips, pushing in to give herself a waist. Her short legs had curves, she thought. They weren't stumps like Betty's. Then she put her hands under her breasts and pushed them up, making them appear bigger. That's what all the boys like, she thought and then quickly dropped her hands as her face turned beet red. She giggled as she always did when embarrassed. She looked down and saw the pencil on the floor. How did that get there, she wondered. She bent over and picked it up. She looked at herself once more, turning left and right. When she did, she thought about Davy. *Someday*, she promised herself.

***

Davy opened his eyes. At least he thought he did. He couldn't see anything. At first he thought he was back in the closet, locked up in the dark. He started to panic, twisting and wrenching his body to wiggle backwards, but just before he started screaming, he felt that same calming feeling from before. This time he didn't associate it with a child. It had a different feel. Then it got light. The ulasiga had locked onto

Davy's optic nerve and began sending a mixture of signals it had put together after it had downloaded his memory.

At first, Davy saw a blurry circle, like a moon, swirling around. Soon his eyes adjusted and the light engulfed the entire area. Davy was in a big room, like the living rooms rich people had, ones he had seen on TV. A stone fireplace, with logs ablaze, filled one wall, although Davy couldn't feel any heat, and a big long white overstuffed couch sat in front of it. A blue plush square rug covered the shiny wooden floor and it looked so very thick and soft. Several big overstuffed chairs, also white, sat on either side. They looked just like the ones Davy loved to sit in at the downtown library. The big room looked empty except for the furniture surrounded by blank white walls. Davy turned his head trying to see the whole room, straining to see above and behind him. The ceiling looked as white and as blank as the walls, no light fixtures or lamps lit the room, yet he could see. Davy tried to walk further into the room but found he couldn't move his arms or legs. He looked behind him, expecting to see the entrance from the cave outside. Instead, he saw another white wall. He turned a full circle without moving his feet and looked back toward the couch. This time he saw someone sitting on it. He blinked rapidly several times and would have rubbed his eyes had he been able to raise his arms.

A little blonde girl sat there with her hands folded in her lap. She wore short red pants and a yellow tee-shirt with a big mouse on it, one that looked somewhat familiar, but not exactly. He recognized her from the store where she had looked at him through those very same sad eyes. Davy had known her pain. Not only had she been sad, but a physical pain he couldn't fix pooled inside her. He immediately began to send her a tickle. As he looked at her, the eyes changed and now he saw that she smiled back. She held a big white stuffed teddy bear with a red bow in her lap. Where had that come from he wondered, but just for a second, because suddenly another child appeared right beside the girl. A boy this time. He looked a little younger than the girl. He was dressed in dirty blue jeans and also had a tee-shirt, this one just plain white. Had he been there all along? His excitement at seeing a familiar face overcame his surprise. The last time he had seen him, he had been playing alone in the sandbox, using one arm to push a big truck, the other tucked into his coat. He too, had those same sad eyes as the girl's. His, too, changed at that very moment and a smile crossed his lips. Then he lifted his arm, the one that had been hidden in the coat when Davy had seen him in the park. It didn't look like it hurt him. There was no bandage.

They both smiled and waved to him. He tried to wave back, but his arms stayed stuck by his sides. He yelled out a hello to them and, still smiling, they went back to playing with their toys, mounds of them now covered the floor and couch. A train sat in the middle of the carpet and it went round and round spouting smoke, its little whistle tooting as it moved. When Davy looked back at the two on the couch, he saw they both held giant lollipops; the ones with all the colors swirled in a circle and as big as their heads. He had seen some just like them in the store. Where had they suddenly come from?

All the while the ulasiga burned energy manipulating brain waves, reacting at lightning speed to what the Davy thought. It wanted the signals clear and perfect so it moved closer. The closer it got, the better the reception. The ulasiga worked fast, taking in the brain waves, interpreting them, then weaving new visions to set the scene. At first the ulasiga had gotten it all wrong and felt the harsh reaction from the Davy's mind. The ulasiga adjusted what the Davy saw until it felt the right wave length coming from him, one that matched the calm state. It could change visual inputs quicker than the Davy could blink. Every time a wave came through that questioned what the ulasiga displayed, it would make quick adjustments, pulling from the Davy's memory what he expected to see. For the ulasiga to use the necessary imagery on this man, it had to expose more of its body.

Davy stood still, watching the children play. Once the surprise wore off, Davy looked around. Other than an occasional whistle from the train, it was very quiet. He tried to find the lamps or lights but all he saw was the white walls. He tried without success to lift his hands closer to the fireplace. He couldn't feel any heat. He began to fidget. He didn't feel right about what he saw. The absolute silence from the children and the fire bothered him the most. He closed his eyes so that he could concentrate on listening. When he did, the scene didn't disappear. Davy became even more confused and frightened. Why hadn't dark come when he closed his eyes? He opened them and everything stayed the same. He tried to reach up and touch his eyelids but his arms wouldn't obey. He focused on the children, still on the couch, still engrossed in play. I'll squeeze my eyes really tight 'til I see colors, like playing hide and seek, he thought. This time he focused and closed them hard. Everything went dark and with relief he re-opened them. Just for a fraction of a second, everything appeared wavy and unfocused, but then it stopped. Davy noticed several lamps and he did smell smoke, not quite fireplace smoke but his attention returned to the children. Had there been this many toys before?

The ulasiga extended more of its body into the cave and hung suspended above the Davy's head. As the man's mind rejected things, the ulasiga searched for the correct feelings and matched the waves, implanting the needed subtle changes. It was fast and draining work that required the ulasiga to contact the man's head. The ulasiga allowed a few cells to touch the man's head. Tiny wisps of smoke rose. The ulasiga blocked what little pain the tiny spots would generate. This man turned out to be more complicated than it had anticipated. For the first time in its long life, the ulasiga completely exposed itself. It had pushed most of its body to the surface to control this man. The speed which it had to work and the energy drain it caused forced the ulasiga to hurry to complete the ploy. Then the ulasiga found a thought that could calm the man.

Davy tried to fit all the pieces of this puzzle together. Not like the big puzzles they had at the group home where Roberta lived, these pieces were small and didn't seem to fit. Davy fought against his own feelings. His confusion turned into a full-fledged panic when Mr. Harrington, his boss from the store walked in. The scene flickered and then Davy felt calm again. Maybe he was dreaming.

"Mr. Harrington? What are you doing here?" Davy asked.

"Hi, Davy," Mr. Harrington replied.

Davy saw that Mr. Harrington wore his normal smile as if he were at work and not in some strange place.

Davy hadn't expected to see his boss. Mr. Harrington was probably one of the few adults that Davy trusted. He had never called him stupid or made fun of him. Whenever Davy got confused, Mr. Harrington would help. Maybe he could explain. Davy watched as Mr. Harrington sat on the couch between the two children and put his arms around them. They both looked up at Mr. Harrington and smiled. Davy knew that smile. It was one he got from the children when he tickled their minds.

"So, you found Protection," Mr. Harrington said.

"Huh?" asked Davy

"Protection. It's what I call this place," he said as he waved his hand around the room. "Protection is my little home for abused children. When I find them, like little Tiffany and Billy, here, I take them away from their parents," he said.

Davy jumped when Mr. Harrington suddenly slammed his hand on the arm of the couch. Davy had never seen him like that. His face became all distorted and angry.

"Oh, how I hate calling them parents. They don't deserve it!"

Mr. Harrington hung his head and shook it slowly. He looked back up at Davy with sad eyes.

"They are monsters, Davy. The real thing. Do you know what happens to children that are hurt by their ..." with a look of foulness he continued, "parents?" He spat the words out like he had eaten something rotten.

Davy nodded. "They turn black inside."

"That's right!" said Mr. Harrington. "Their spirit killed by the very people who are supposed to protect them!"

"But Mr. Harrington," said Davy. "When I showed you that boy in the store, you didn't do anything."

"I couldn't Davy. I wanted to, I really did, but I can't be exposed. If people knew I took these children, abused or not, I would go to jail. Then where would these children be?"

Davy didn't know what to say. He stared at Mr. Harrington, who now looked different and much taller, taller than in the store. It made him a bit uncomfortable.

"You can help me, Davy," he said.

"I can? How?" he asked.

Davy brushed at the goose bumps along his arms and neck.

"You know when you see abused children, you can feel it. You can talk to them in their minds where parents can't. You could find a way to bring them here to Protection, where nothing will ever hurt them again."

"Isn't it against the law?"

"Only if you get caught. You'd be saving their lives, saving them from pain. Nobody else can help. Nobody can see their pain the way you can," said Mr. Harrington. Davy saw a tear roll down Mr. Harrington's cheek.

Davy held very still as he thought about that, looking for the right and wrong of it. He looked at Mr. Harrington who now looked at him in a way he had never seen before, sad, and anxious. He let his eyes wander to the boy and girl, happy and smiling. He had seen the TV police chase people that stole children. But those bad people had meant to hurt children. He would be saving them. Saving someone was right. He knew that. He looked back at the children on the couch. He looked at the smiles and felt the wholeness inside of them. Would he do it? Could he do it?

He thought about the store, the parents rushing down the aisles ignoring their children, the park, the places where it had felt the sadness of the children. Maybe he could. He thought about the faces, the hurt, the pain, the dark places, the pleading looks from the children. Yes, he would do it!

"I think I can," Davy said. "If you help me."

"No Davy, I can't help. In fact, you can't even talk to me about it outside of here. You have to pretend you never even saw me and I'll pretend I never saw you. Remember, if we get caught, if you say anything, all these children, all the ones we can save, will have to stay with their parents. You wouldn't want that would you?"

"No sir," said Davy. "But how will I get them to come?"

"Use your mind, Davy," said Mr. Harrington. "Like you told me. You can find them and when you can, sneak them away and bring them here."

"Why me, Mr. Harrington? I'm just a dumb old stock boy."

"Don't ever say that. You're special, Davy. Don't you know you are the only one in the whole world that can do this? Because we're finding and saving children, we have to keep it a secret. Someday, when we have saved enough, we'll be able to tell and then you'll be a big hero, but not yet. You have to keep it quiet. Can you do that?"

"Yes, sir, but if I can get one to come here, how will I find this place again?"

"Don't worry. You will. Just think hard and you'll be able to walk right to it."

"Are you sure Mr. Harrington? Is this right?"

"We have to do this Davy. I'll do it with or without you. What other choice is there? Look at these two! You remember their pain. Are they hurting now?"

Davy thought about it. He did remember and he remembered his own. "What if I goof and say something?"

"They won't believe you will they, Davy? They'll treat you like they always have; like you're a dummy. Like you're not important. You know how they are."

Davy thought about that and remembered the teasing and laughter. He remembered the wedgies from the other boys. He remembered the man on the trail. Nobody would listen to a dumb old stock boy.

"Now Davy, it's time to go, you close your eyes and I'm going to turn off the lights. You won't be able to see or hear us when you open them up. Crawl back out and go home. If you see a child hurting, convince him to come here. Tell him of the other children, tell him of the toys, but only bring one a month. Too many and people will get suspicious."

"Okay, Mr. Harrington. But what if—"

Davy eyes closed by themselves and when he opened them, the dark had returned. He felt his way back to the opening and began to wiggle his way out of the hole. He felt a trickle of pain, like a fine hair ran across his neck. It burned, but it didn't really hurt.

***

The ulasiga had been manipulating the Davy's brain waves as fast as it could, both receiving and sending signals. When it finally read acceptance, it put its own memory inside. Although not as powerful as close connection, it hoped it would be enough to assure the big man's return.

It had infiltrated the Davy's memory and filtered through all the information stored there including the cop shows and mysteries that the Davy watched. It had found all the emotions that motivated the Davy and integrated them into the memory implanted. It also pulled from memory, things that even the man couldn't access. The ulasiga found the fears from the man, being lost, and it bolstered them enough to ensure the man could remember the path home and the return trip. The ulasiga disconnected. It felt a chill from the loss of the activity. It felt the vibrations as the Davy crawled from the cave. The ulasiga returned to its lair, picturing the children that this man would bring back.

It returned to feed from its stores and rest and to review its work. It didn't want to let the Davy go. He carried memories and pictures that the ulasiga had never seen. But the possibility of having a steady source of food outweighed the possibility that this would not work.

EIGHT

Davy felt surprised how easily he found the trail home. He even knew which direction to go when he got there. The splashes marking the way remained ignored as were the squirrels and birds. Even the people he passed went by unnoticed, except for the children. He still saw the children. He walked quickly and lightly down the trail, his mind racing with what had just happened to him.

Back at home he turned his chair in the living room in the direction of the cave, toward 'Protection'. He knew that it lay that way and he could even picture the pathway there. He saw the big room, the soft carpet and huge chairs. He could imagine the place filled with happy, smiling children. He could imagine being in the center and playing with them.

He closed his eyes and tried to imagine the faces of all the children he had ever met, especially the ones with that sad, hurt look, the look that would tell him they needed to go to 'Protection.' He couldn't believe Mr. Harrington had enlisted him. The trust made Davy's chest swell. He remembered how good he felt when he first started working and Mr. Harrington had given him an assignment alone. Now Mr. Harrington had given him a job bigger than anything he ever did in the store. More important than pricing; more important than stacking glass jars. Davy couldn't believe how good he felt. He strutted around his apartment with a huge smile on his face.

Davy's ringing phone brought him out of his musings. "Hello, This is Davy," he answered.

"Where have you been? I'm stuck in this stupid house, with these stupid people, trying to do this stupid homework," Roberta said loud enough that Davy had to pull the receiver away from his ear.

"Hi, Roberta. How are you doing? What's a matter? You have a fight or something?"

"Not really. Betty was being a butthead."

"Well that's okay. Just forget about it. So what do you want?"

"I'm trying to find out the name of those long noodle things."

"Sure, spaghetti, aisle six."

"Duh! I must be stupid. Spaghetti. I knew it."

"That's okay. I forget the names, too, sometimes. "

"Yea, and you're the stupid stock boy," she laughed.

"Oh yea? You're just a stupid girl."

"Yea, that's right," she said. "A stupid girl in this stupid house."

Davy felt her disappointment. He remembered how he felt living there day after day, wondering if he would ever learn enough to move out on his own. He still had lists stuck up everywhere in his place to remind him of things he had to do.

"Do you have any other homework I can help you with?" he asked.

"Help me with one thing and now you think you're smarter than the whole world. Stupid stock boy," she said.

Davy heard the anger through the phone.

"I'm not a stupid stock boy," he said. "I'm special. I have other responsibilities!" he said.

"Oh, yeah? Like what stupid stock boy? Are you in charge of the bathrooms?"

"No! I save children …," and Davy quickly stopped. He remembered a little of what Mr. Harrington had said. Now he wished he had kept his mouth shut, but that Roberta, she could be so … so … crazy, was the only word he could come up with.

"You what? Save children? From what?"

"Nothing," he faked a laugh. "I was just picking on you. Sorry."

"Davy, you're so dumb sometimes."

Davy dropped into his chair, relieved that Roberta hadn't asked more. He really wanted to tell someone of his new special responsibilities.

"Takes one to know one," he said.

Roberta laughed at that.

"I got to go spaghetti head," she said and hung up.

Davy set his phone down and began to worry. Could he really do what he promised?

***

Roberta went back to her room and wrote spaghetti on her list before she forgot again. She thought about what Davy had said, how he saved children. She wished she could save children, or anyone for that matter. All she had was this dumb old boring life of making lists and putting up with meanies like Betty. Maybe if Davy saved children, she could help him.

She could imagine herself in red tights with a cape, battling monsters to save a school bus full of children. Then she thought of the tiny babies she saw on her trips to the stores and malls. A wonderful feeling came over her, one like what she felt when she got near Davy, just a little different. She couldn't put her finger on it. She imagined holding her own baby, tight to her chest. Then she could see the giant monster coming to attack. She felt heat building up inside her and pressure in her chest, her anger exploding through body as she grabbed the creature by the throat and flung it across the entire city. Roberta snapped out of her fantasy and smiled. She could protect children. She would ask Davy after the 'Independent Living Classes' later in the week what he had meant when he said he saved children. Roberta wrote it down.

***

Davy went to bed and tried to sleep, but the day's events kept him awake. At first he'd feel powerful, like cartoon superheroes surrounded by crowds of cheering people. Then he would remember what Mr. Harrington had said, how he had to keep quiet. There would be no cheering crowd. He remembered the angry man on the trail, how mean he looked. What would he have done to Davy? But then again, that man loved his boy. These people didn't want their children. Why else would they beat them? Would they even care if they disappeared? Davy couldn't clearly read adults, but he could sense the conflict within them, the ones that hurt their children. Davy knew firsthand about getting beat and then hugged, about being stuffed in a dark closet for hours and then caressed. Davy tossed and turned all night while dreams wove in and out, sometimes the hero, sometimes the villain.

***

Justin Bailey, dressed in his Spiderman pajamas, hid under his bed. He looked up at the springs, wondering if he could grab on to them and hold himself off the floor just like the real Spiderman. He didn't feel powerful enough and he didn't have Spiderman's web. Still, his Spidy sense worked fine. Extreme danger moved in his direction and steadily came closer. He had left himself no escape. He could hear his mother bellowing for him from the kitchen. He recognized the thickness in her voice and the way her letters ran together. It meant only one thing. She was drunk. He knew something else. He would probably go to bed with a whipping. He wondered whether to go now and get whatever she had planned, or stay here and hope she passed out before she found him. The longer he waited, the more dangerous it became because the level of beating grew with the time it took to find him.

He listened to her yell again and tried to judge which way she moved. He also knew she had several moods when drunk and he tried to guess which one. He could jump in bed and fake sleep, or he could try to escape to another room. Maybe he could go in the bathroom and pretend to be pooping. He squeezed his butt cheeks and felt the deep pain inside from the whippings. It extended all the way up to his tiny shoulder blades and down to the back of his knees. It felt sore to the bone and he could almost feel the blows being laid down on top of the deep bruises already there. He curled into the fetal position and began to cry.

He heard her voice again, this time moving. He lifted his head quickly and wiped the tears away. Now he no longer had a decision to make. Once she left the kitchen, he had to hide because she rarely passed out when she raged through the house. Justin sniffed away the snot that had formed below his nose and wiped the residue on his sleeve. He slid further under the bed, placing his back against the wall, pushing into it as tightly as he could. He looked up at the mattress springs and again wished he could attach himself to the bottom, just like Spiderman. The door to his room exploded open and slammed into the wall behind it. Light washed under the bed, broken by two shadows, his mother's legs. Justin froze.

Anger and resentment consumed Mary. She had been sitting in the kitchen, having a few drinks and going over her bills, which significantly exceeded her checkbook balance. She had called for Justin. She just wanted to show him what a no good father he had. The bastard had left without so much as a toodle-do, leaving her with the bills he had racked up and a kid that ate like a Pac Man.

"Justin!"

She stood there looking about his messy room. Clothes lay everywhere, clothes she had bought and the bill for them sat right on the table. She would show him that bill as well. She yelled loud enough to be heard in every room in the house.

"Justin! Come here right now!"

Just like his father. He would disappear whenever she wanted him. She wouldn't be ignored. Not in this life! She may not be able to drag his stinking father to the table, but Justin belonged to her and he would do what she said.

"Justin! You're about 5 minutes from an ass whipping!"

Justin forced himself deeper into the crack. He had fallen for that trick once before and had come out from the closet only to take a beating anyway. Once committed, he had to stay the course. He closed his eyes hard and tried to wish her away. Instead, he imagined the twisted angry look that would be on her face as she stood in his doorway, feet spread to keep her from staggering too much. He knew she held the chunk of broom handle she'd use. He could hear her explanation as she told him that his ass was too hard for her hand to make an impression.

His ears pricked up when he heard her feet turn and walk away. She left the room and her footsteps went down the hall. He heard her bump into the wall, knocking a picture off.

"Sonofabitch! Rotten no good son of a no good father! Justin! Goddamnit!" she hollered from just outside his door.

Justin held his ground as he listened to her going through the other rooms. A door slammed. Her footsteps echoed down the hall then disappeared as she went into a carpeted room. He slowly shifted his position on the hardwood floor. The cold was coming through his pajamas. He hoped she would soon tire and sit down in the kitchen. It had worked before. All the yelling would make her hoarse and she'd take a break from her rampage. He listened to see if he could hear her in the kitchen. If he heard the bottle clink on glass it may be the last he heard. He prayed for it now. He strained to hear her movements. He couldn't locate her. The house had gone silent. Had he missed the sounds of her in the kitchen? He tried to hear the mumbling that often came as she refilled her glass. Perhaps he had missed it this time or maybe she had sat down on her bed and passed out. He remembered all the times he had found her in there splayed on the bed. When he found her like that, he would try to straighten her out and cover her, hoping the act of kindness would calm her. Justin let his body relax as he imagined her in there now, sleeping. He would survive another night. He started to drop off to sleep.

"Justin!"

His eyes flew open. The voice sounded like it came from right next to him. Suddenly, the light invaded his hiding spot as his mattress flew off the bed. He closed his eyes and curled into the tightest ball he could make.

"Get out from under there you little rat," she hissed in a drunken slur. "You come when I call, unnerstand?"

He felt her hand latch around his wrist and she began dragging him up from the floor. He reached out and grabbed the leg of the bed, holding as tight as he could.

"God damn you, you little son of a bastard!" she screamed.

He felt her give a hard jerk on his arm and he lost his grip when something in his shoulder gave out. At eight, Justin was no match for his mother and knew it. He went back into a ball. Time slowed for Justin. It felt to him like it took forever for the first blow to land. He let out no screams when the wood handle struck him, nor any after. Justin found himself in a life and death struggle and his best defense was to keep locked in his ball as the blows continued. Each blow came with a bolt of fire that traveled the full length of his body. He felt the pain radiate through fresh bruises into old bruises, heavy and metallic. The sharp waves shot through him right to the base of his skull. He felt one glance off his backbone and it made ears pop. Tears flooded his eyes. He kept his teeth clamped tight as he prepared for the next one. Up above him, he heard the grunting and swearing as his mother tried to line up another shot through a drunk's eyes.

Mary tried to keep her attack to Justin's backside, just as her father had done to her, but Justin's struggle and her drunkenness caused more than a few to go astray. Finally, her resolve dissipated and her anger abated. She stood, swaying, and looked down at the ball at her feet. He should have come when I called, she told herself. She turned and walked out of his room without a word, closing the door behind her. She returned to the kitchen and refilled her glass.

Justin remained in his position for a long time. He worried she may come back refreshed and renew the beating. When he finally had to move, he straightened out slowly knowing the hurts old and new would reveal themselves with shooting pain. Finally he crawled back under the bed and leaned his back against the cool wall. The cold helped ease the hurt. Then the tears really began. Not just for the hurt, but knowing the beatings would never stop.

NINE

Mr. Harrington began to worry about Davy. Over the last few days Davy hadn't been acting normally. He had lost his smile and barely acknowledged the other employees when they passed by him in the aisles. He had even made several uncharacteristic mistakes while stocking shelves and missed his break more than once. Mr. Harrington finally called him into his office and closed the door.

"Davy, is everything all right?"

"Yes sir, Mr. Harrington," Davy said. He kept his gaze on the floor.

"Are you sure? You have been acting a little strange the last few days. I haven't seen you smile or even wave."

"I'm sorry. I guess I've been thinking about things."

"What things? Is there anything I can help you with?"

Davy looked up at him. He of all people should know. Davy wanted to tell him that he had been worried about making a mistake, perhaps letting the secret out or even mistaking a child's feelings and taking the wrong one. He wanted to tell him about the pressure of keeping the secret. He needed to talk about it. And he worried because he hadn't found any children that needed his help.

This could be a test, Davy suddenly thought. He held his tongue. Inwardly it made him feel a little better. Just having Mr. Harrington call him in for a private meeting made him feel less alone. He would pass this test. He wouldn't say anything about their meeting in the cave. The thought made him smile and he saw that it made Mr. Harrington smile. That satisfied Davy. Still, the need to share his secret persisted. He had so many questions about what to do. When and how soon, and how would Mr. Harrington know when he had taken one so he wouldn't have to leave him alone? He had almost too many things to consider.

"That's better," Mr. Harrington told him. "You're special Davy. Sometimes you will be faced with difficulties, but I know you can get through anything. Just keep that smile."

"Uh, yes sir, Mr. Harrington. Thanks."

Davy stood for a moment and then went back to mopping floors. He thought about what Mr. Harrington said. It was an obvious code, like the spy movies used, Mr. Harrington's way of telling him that he could handle it. Davy felt even more important. The pressure that had been building inside, screaming for him to tell someone eased, yet it hovered like an itch he couldn't quite reach.

***

Roberta paced around in her room. Tonight, the Independent Living Class met and she would get to see Davy for the first time since she talked to him on the phone. She wasn't entirely sure what she wanted to ask. She remembered very little of what they talked about. She had to look at her list just to remember the name of those long skinny noodles. She had written beside it, 'Davy saves little kids.' She looked at it now. She would ask Davy if he would show her how she could save some, too. She looked in the mirror and began to brush her short black hair. The brush went easily through it, tickling her scalp as she raked it across her head. She smiled at herself in the mirror and then frowned. She could easily see that she looked different from normal people. It felt like she had a sign that said 'Look at me, I'm stupid.'

Roberta put her head on her crossed arms and began to cry. Why couldn't she be normal, she wondered. What did I do to deserve this?

Roberta recalled earlier days when she had a real mother and not just a string of people that tried to play the part. She had been a princess then. Some of the other kids had talked about a father, but she hadn't known hers or why he wasn't there while she grew up. She had some memories of earlier years when she was about seven. That was before she really noticed that she looked different from the other children. Her mother had called her special and she had believed it. She even went to a school with other special children and she spent the days playing and laughing. Life had been just fine.

One day after Roberta turned thirteen, some strangers met her at school. They told her that her mother had gone to see God. They brought her to a big house where they let her see her mother. Roberta felt unnerved by the bright lights and all the shiny metal in the place. She wanted to reach up and plug her nose against the smell that burned and made her eyes water.

The two people that had escorted her from the school led her across the room where she found her mother sleeping on a big metal table. But she noticed right away that it wasn't her mother. Some fake woman made to look like her mother lay there. Her mother looked shinier than that, even when she slept. Still, the man and woman had taken her away and she never saw her mother again. Roberta couldn't remember much of what happened after that.

When her crying subsided, she glanced into the mirror again. Now her eyes looked wet and red, too, drawing even more attention to them.

She hated those eyes and she glared at them hatefully. An instant pain struck as if someone jabbed their fingers into them. She slammed her eyes shut and covered them with her hands. When the pain stopped she rubbed them; not wanting to look again, fearing they would look even worse. She kept her eyes closed tight as her frustration continued.

She thought about the happy TV families. Would she ever get to have one? Would she ever be a mother? She knew she was different from others, this thing they call Down syndrome, but they said it could be overcome. She had tried, really tried, but it didn't seem to get better. She wanted out of here, out of this house. She wanted away from Betty. She wished she could live with Davy. Together, they would be fine.

Then her thoughts faded and she realized she was sitting at her desk, eyes squeezed closed. She opened them again. Her reflection had turned blurry in the mirror. Worried that she may be losing her vision, she blinked rapidly a number of times and slowly her eyesight began to clear up. Relieved, she got up and walked down the hall to the bathroom. There she splashed water on her face and dried it with a towel, already forgetting what had happened. The cool wetness helped calm her and she returned to her room. By the time she sat down and picked up her shopping list, what had just happened faded.

***

Davy couldn't keep his mind on the activities during the Independent Living Class. His thoughts were on the house in the mountains and the children safe inside. They were his mission, his responsibility. All the chatter bounced off the edge of his consciousness, barely making it in his head. Even though he saw Roberta looking at him all through the class, it barely registered. Davy plotted out his course of action.

 Roberta looked at Davy. He normally sat up in his seat, smiling. Today, he slunk down in his chair. He didn't even smile back when Roberta smiled at him. She tried a different tact, frowning and making faces. Nothing. She wondered if he was mad at her.

Mrs. Anderson, the house supervisor, had to call his name several times before she got a response from the normally alert Davy. When she asked him what number to call if he smelled smoke, Davy just looked at her like she hadn't said a word. As she continued the lesson, she noticed that he stared out the window or down at his hands. She made a mental note to talk with him later, after class. There had to be an explanation for his mood. As the class wore on, the rest of the household members caught his mood and began acting out. It got like that sometimes. Arguments and flare ups occurred between people even when they weren't the ones acting strange. Mrs. Anderson ended the class early with new homework assignments; listing important phone numbers and names. She asked Davy to come to her office after class.

"What's wrong Davy?"

"Nothing, Mrs. Anderson."

"Well, you're pretty distracted tonight. You couldn't even answer simple questions. Do you feel okay?"

"Yes, Mrs. Anderson."

"Have you been taking your medicine? Things at work are okay?"

"Yes."

"If there is something I can help you with, you'll let me know, won't you?"

Davy looked at Mrs. Anderson carefully. Besides Mr. Harrington, she was just about the nicest person Davy knew. She had been there the whole time he lived in the house. She had actually helped him move out. Surely he could tell her about Protection. Davy started to speak, but before any words could come out, his throat tightened and an image of Mr. Harrington in the cave came to mind.

"No, Mrs. Anderson. Everything's just great. Maybe I'm coming down with a cold."

Mrs. Anderson ruffled his hair and stood up.

"All right then. As long as you're fine, I'll leave you alone. You promise that if anything's wrong you'll tell me."

"Yes ma'am."

Davy left Mrs. Anderson's office and saw Roberta standing there. Seeing her lightened his mood as he momentarily forgot his problem. He liked her a lot, but he didn't know how to go about expressing it.

"Hey, Roberta" he said.

"Hey yourself. What ya doin'?"

"Oh Mrs. Anderson just wanted to talk. Did you get your list finished?"

"Yeah. Those stupid noodles. You going home now?"

"In a minute. I just want to see who's around."

Actually Davy wanted to stay as long as he could. Talking to Roberta, or anyone else, for that matter, kept his mind off his mission. The thought that maybe Roberta would like to go to Protection with him, maybe live there like he planned to do, jumped up and down in his head. The thought instantly tickled his insides and made his heart seem extra large.

Then he quickly dismissed the idea. He had a purpose and a trust to fulfill. Maybe he would ask Mr. Harrington about it the next time he saw him there.

"Hey, Davy," Roberta whispered. "I want to save children, too."

Davy looked at her and then quickly up and down the hall to see if anyone had heard. He looked back at Roberta, surprised she had remembered, afraid because she might be blabbing it to the whole house.

"Listen Roberta, I was just joking. I was making stuff up."

Roberta looked at Davy.

"No, Davy. I know you're lying."

"I am not."

"Davy, please. Come on. I can help. I can do something. I'm not stupid."

Davy looked at Roberta. He saw the deep hurt inside her. He could read her like the children at the store. He would have calmed her, but something inside of her always blocked his signals. He remembered how he had felt, how lonely and useless until Mr. Harrington gave him some trust. Maybe he could let Roberta in on a little, just a tiny bit so she could feel important, too.

Davy looked up and down the hall again. Seeing nobody there, he leaned in close and whispered in her ear.

"Can you keep a secret?"

Roberta nodded her head yes.

"I'm looking out for children, kids that have been hurt by their parents."

Roberta stared at him. "Where do you look for them?"

"At my store and at the park, sometimes when I'm on the bus."

"How do you know they're hurt? Bandages?"

"I can just tell."

"What do you do if you find them?" she asked.

"I try to help them."

"How?"

"I can't tell. I just help them so they aren't hurt anymore," Davy said as he scanned the hallway for people that might be listening.

"Can I do it, too?"

"No!" he said. He saw the pain run from her eyes to her face so he quickly added, "You're too far away to help them, but maybe you can help me. I might need someone to call the police if I can't help them. Could you do that?"

Roberta stepped back a few paces and looked at Davy again. This time her eyes went wide as saucers. Then she looked up and down the hall. "Are you crazy? Call the police? What would I say?"

Davy just looked at her, his mind racing too fast to answer. Inside he cringed at what he had asked, now too late to take back. Roberta got excited, though, and that made him feel better. Roberta thought his pause meant impatience so she continued.

"What's the number? What would I say?" she asked.

"Shsss! Roberta! Nobody can know!"

"Okay! I'll help," she whispered.

"Only if you promise. A double special promise to not tell."

"I promise. How will I know when to call? What should I say?"

"I'll tell you when the time comes."

Davy wanted to say more. He ached inside. He felt like he would burst if he didn't let it out. He forced his mind to recapture the house, the scene inside, and Mr. Harrington laying his hand on his shoulder and telling him how important Davy was to the mission. The small bit he had confided to Roberta had relieved some of the pressure, although Davy actually hoped she would soon forget what he had told her.

TEN

Davy saw many children over the next several days. Only one felt as though he may need his help. The small, pale three year old riding in the cart with his mother had that aura. At first Davy thought the boy was just mad for some unknown reason so he tried to tickle him with his mind. The small boy looked at him with a half smile. He felt something wrong and Davy moved closer, pretending to stack boxes. When he opened his mind to the young child's feelings, he could sense the pain and fear. He could feel the hurt inside, some physical, but mostly a mental anguish that Davy saw as a black cloud. Davy carefully followed them around the store, up and down each aisle. He looked for an opportunity. Would the mother leave the boy unattended or could he distract her? He mentally pictured all the exits. The one at the front had too many people coming in and out. He could visualize the loading dock where the truck drivers and forklift guys worked. That wouldn't work this time of day. He looked up and saw the black bubble that hid the store cameras. He knew he would never get away. He knew he wouldn't be able to do anything here at the store. He tried to memorize the boy's face and hoped he would see him again somewhere else.

Once he decided to let this one go, Davy had to run to the back of the store and into the bathroom. He had to sit on the toilet to keep from falling. His knees shook and his stomach spun. He watched his shaky hands reach out and turn on the faucet so he could splash cold water on his face. He saw a strange person looking at him in the mirror, wide eyed and pale. Several minutes went by before he could force himself to leave the safety of the small room.

Davy found that as the days got shorter, even the parks became deserted. Winter would be along soon. He began to feel an urgency to complete his task, a need to find a child he could help, but it couldn't be a child from the store. He decided he would have to go where the children were, schools and daycares. Davy had seen enough police shows to know he had to make sure nobody noticed him. Maybe Roberta would go for a walk with him on Saturday and he could take her by the schools to look for places where he could see the children without being noticed, where he wouldn't stand out.

Roberta's heart did a little jump when she got the call from Davy, thinking he would ask her to call the police as he had told her earlier. Her opportunity to do her part to save children had come. When he asked her to go for a walk instead, she frowned, but wondered if he would reveal more secrets or ask her to help in other ways. Either way, it didn't matter. Roberta loved being able to leave the house and she would make sure dumb old Betty knew Davy had asked her.

Roberta, anxiously waiting for Davy to arrive, paced the hall by the front door of the house. As soon as she saw him on the sidewalk outside, Roberta headed for the door.

"Roberta!" said Mrs. Anderson. "Where do you think you're going?"

"Davy's here."

"You know you have to wait until he comes in. You are not allowed outside without signing out and permission," Mrs. Anderson said.

"But you said I could go," said Roberta.

"That's right, but you still have to follow the rules. Davy has to come in and sign out with you," she said.

"Yes, ma'am," Roberta said.

Davy knocked and Roberta let him in.

"Hi, Roberta," said Davy.

"Hey," said Roberta.

"Hello, Davy," said Mrs. Anderson.

"Hi, Mrs. Anderson, how are you today?" Davy asked.

"I'm fine Davy. Where are you taking Roberta and how long will you be gone?"

"I think we will just go down the street two or three blocks and back. Maybe we'll get some ice cream, too. How long can she stay out?"

"Can you be back by lunch?"

"Sure," Davy said.

"Okay. Sign out first. We'll see you two at twelve."

Once they left the group home and walked down the sidewalk, Roberta pressed Davy for more details about saving children. Davy could never understand why Roberta could remember some things and not others. At first, he tried to resist. He tried to distract Roberta, then he tried to ignore her. When that didn't work, he tried telling her it was too dangerous for her to know. Instead of being scared, she pressed harder.

"You know, Davy, I love children, too. I thought that someday you and me could have a baby of our own. I mean once I'm out of that house."

Davy stopped dead and turned toward Roberta who looked at the sidewalk. She had turned a bright red. Davy reached out and gave her a clumsy hug. Roberta returned it for just a second and then pushed him away.

"Not here." She said.

"I'm sorry," said Davy. "It was just a hug. You won't have babies from just a hug."

"That's how it starts."

"Well, can I hold your hand?"

"Yes, if that's all you do," replied Roberta, now all prim and proper.

They continued to walk for a while and Davy let the thought of fatherhood race around in his mind, his mission put on the back burner until Roberta spoke again.

"You can trust me, Davy."

"Roberta, look at me. Stare into my eyes."

Roberta looked at Davy and then shifted her eyes away, smiling and embarrassed. Davy took both of her hands.

"If you want to know, you have to see what I can do. You have to look at me for it to work. This is not a game Roberta, this is serious."

"I thought you were playing stare down. I'm sorry. I wish I wasn't so stupid!"

"You're not stupid Roberta," Davy said quietly. "Now look at me and relax."

Roberta looked into Davy's eyes, narrowing her focus to just the blue and then even further into the black. She began to feel a tickle inside, around her ribs, gentle and warm, and it made her smile. Then she saw him look away and the feeling left."

"I can't see your eyes. You moved them away."

"That was it," he said. "I guess you didn't feel it, but I saw you smile."

"Feel what? What did you do? I always smile when I see you, goofy."

"I can tickle people just by thinking about it, at least children can feel it all the time. I can make them feel good and I can feel when they feel bad."

"That was you?"

"You felt it? It was me that did it."

"I felt good but how do I know it was you? You didn't do anything but look at me."

Davy flared. "I did too!"

Roberta stepped back shocked by the sudden anger.

"I'm sorry," said Davy. "Come on, I'll show you."

Davy took Roberta to a nearby supermarket. He knew he could find children in grocery stores. Once inside they walked around until Davy found a little girl sitting in a cart with tears. Her mother was telling her no, as the child reached for the plush stuffed animals. Davy took Roberta's arm.

"Stay right behind me and watch that little girl."

Davy grabbed the nearest stuffed animal off the shelf and shook it to gain the little girl's attention. Like all children she looked at the motion and then at Davy. Anxious to prove his point, he sent a wave to the girl, a little stronger than usual. The little girl jumped just a tiny bit as the jolt hit her. She quickly wrapped her arms around her middle and started giggling. Davy quickly turned around and pulled Roberta away as the mother turned to see what caused her child to laugh.

Davy hurried Roberta down the opposite aisle and across the store. Roberta kept turning around trying to see the little girl as Davy urged her on. Finally he got her out of the store and he started walking rapidly across the parking lot.

"Wow! Davy, did you do that? I want to see it again. Do it again. Do me!"

"I knew I shouldn't have shown you. Now you're going to blab it to everyone."

"But Davy, that is so good. Everybody should know."

"If they do, then I won't be able to help anyone. It has to be a secret!"

"Why?"

"'Cause that's how I find the children that aren't loved anymore. If people know I can find them, they'll keep them in the house and I won't be able to help them. You have to keep it quiet, please!"

Roberta thought about it, at least she tried. She saw the serious expression on Davy's face. If she wanted to help, if she wanted to be special, she should do what he asked.

"Okay. I won't say anything."

"Nothing, not even hints!"

"Okay."

Davy looked at her and felt the will drain right out of him. Roberta wouldn't be able to help herself. The whole house would know within a few days unless she forgot and she didn't seem to be forgetting about the children. Now he would have to be more careful than ever and he didn't have much time. He wanted to take as many children to Protection as he could before the winter closed the trail or Roberta ruined his chances. He walked Roberta back to the house. He stopped at the gate.

"Please don't tell anyone," Davy said.

"I won't," Roberta said.

Davy leaned in quickly and kissed her on the cheek. He turned bright red by the time he backed away. Roberta laid her hand across the spot of the kiss, also turning red.

"Davy," she said.

"What?"

Roberta tried to be mad but couldn't stop the grin. Instead, she turned and ran to the house. She turned and smiled before going through the door.

***

Justin knew it was early; too early to leave for school, but the sooner he could get out of his house the better. Someday he would never have to go back, he thought. He would run away or maybe one of the nice teachers at his school would take him. He quietly dressed in blue jeans and a sweatshirt with the Hulk, all green and muscles, flying through the air. He moved as silently as he could so he wouldn't wake his mother. He had counted several days now without a beating, but if the normal pattern continued, it wouldn't be long before the next one. He would know when, too. The mood in the house would change. His mom would yell a little more often and she would start spending more time at the kitchen table where she would be looking at papers and drinking from a big glass. When she finally quit trying to hide it and left the bottle sitting on the table, Justin knew it wouldn't be long. He wanted to find it and pour it out, but he had done that once before. It had cost him.

Once she got in that mood, alternating between crying and cussing, once the music got loud and she sang off key to sad songs, when she sat staring at the table and the papers on it, Justin knew time wasn't on his side. She would write on a pad and then cuss at the papers and Justin's dad. The volume crept up the longer she sat there. Then she would write some more. She would drink and refill the glass in-between the swearing and the writing. When he would hear his name in the same sentence with his dad's, he knew the time was coming. Sometimes she would crumple the papers and throw them. Sometimes she would sweep the table clean with her arm. Either way, it was bad news. Justin thought that the beatings had become progressively worse. When those signs appeared, Justin would slink off and hide as far away as possible. If he had any place to run, he would have.

For right now, he needed to get out of the house before she woke up. She never beat him in the morning, but she could start her rants at any time and if she started early, she would be on fire when he got home. He crept out into the kitchen and eased open the refrigerator. His mom sat at the kitchen table with her head down on her arms, sleeping. Glass jars and bottles in the fridge rattled. His mother groaned and turned her head. He paused and hoped she would go back to sleep. After a moment, he grabbed a prepackaged lunch and a juice carton. He closed the door as silently as possible. He watched his mother closely when the handle clicked shut. He held his breath as he tiptoed out, freezing when a board squeaked and his mother groaned as she shifted her position. When she settled back down, he pulled on his coat and slipped quietly through the front door. It wasn't until he made sure it was latched and stepped quietly down the creaky porch steps that he could breathe again. He ran down the street toward the school. He would be the first one there, as always. At that time in the morning, he had to use the janitor's door around the back.

ELEVEN

Davy dressed early and instead of going to work, he got on the number 4 bus. Work would come later in the afternoon. He got off at Elm and Front Street, five blocks from the school he picked out. It would be several hours before he would have to leave for work and by then his task here would be finished. He sat down on the bench at the bus stop across the street from Lincoln Elementary and opened up a newspaper. He wanted to appear like he was reading it while he watched the children walk past on their way to school. Looking up and down the street, he didn't see any children about and very little traffic. He looked across the street at the school trying to see children moving behind the windows. Had he picked a holiday? He tried to remember but he didn't know. Stupid, stupid, stupid, he mumbled to himself, angry that his mind wouldn't tell him anything. Would he even see any little kids before he would have to catch the bus to work?

He had only been there for several minutes and it seemed like hours. He looked up and down both sides of the street and didn't see a single person. He lifted his paper higher in case someone watched him from inside one of the houses nearby.

***

Just a block down the street and across the road sat Justin's school. Justin walked with his head down, thinking not of his recent escape, but his eventual return. When he took a moment to look up, he saw a man with his back to him sitting at the bus stop on his side of the street. He paused for just a moment, considering whether to cross over to the other side or walk on by. He didn't see any one else around and no cars either. He decided he would watch the man carefully and, if the man started to come after him, Justin would run as fast as he could to the school. He continued walking but a little slower, not taking his eyes off the person on the bench.

***

Davy didn't hear the small boy approach as much as he felt his presence. He could feel a wave of something, indefinable. Davy thought it felt like a rubber band pulled tight and ready to snap. The fearful feeling came from behind him and moved slowly in his direction. Davy held still, keeping the paper up. When the boy got beside him, Davy slowly turned his head toward him and began to smile. He saw the boy looking at him, the emotion he felt, the tightness in the child grew to a breaking point. He sent his tickle. He instantly felt the tension slip away, but what he found inside shocked him and for the first time ever he broke contact.

***

Justin saw the man's head start to turn in his direction. He coiled; ready to race away if the man started to get up. He had been taught not to look directly at strangers, but he couldn't help himself. Justin saw his face and realized this guy wasn't a regular stranger. He had a round face and big round eyes. He looked at him with a goofy grin. He wasn't scary at all. He seemed more like a big kid than a man. Justin smiled without really knowing why and began to raise his hand to wave. For the first time in a long while, he felt good. Then the man's smile vanished. The man sat back like someone had kicked him. Justin felt the warmth leave at the same time as the man jumped. He got ready to run again, but before he could, that shocked look quickly evaporated and that silly smile returned. Justin felt the good feeling inside return as quickly as the smile had. With the happiness back, he stood there, smiling himself, holding his hand halfway up.

***

Davy regained control quickly. He had felt the blackness inside the child, more than he had ever experienced before. He found it coated the child almost completely. The pain actually rolled through him, leaving a metallic taste in his mouth and an electric feeling on his bones like when he once bit into the tinfoil on a stick of gum. He actually shivered. Quickly, he doubled his efforts in sending warmth and joy into the child. He saw the boy's smile return.

"Hi," said Davy.

Justin just lifted his hand the rest of the way and then dropped it down to his side.

"You go to school here?" asked Davy.

"Yeah," replied Justin. Although he knew he shouldn't be talking to him. Somehow this guy didn't seem dangerous.

"I didn't go to a school like this," Davy said. "Mine was little and only had five or six kids in it."

"There's a whole bunch that go here," said Justin, hitching his thumb over his shoulder toward the school. He did it without taking his eyes off Davy. Besides, I'm fast and this guy could never catch me, he thought. He somehow felt safe around this man like he didn't anywhere else. Anyway, the school sat right across the street and other children would come soon so it wasn't like there wasn't anyone else around.

"It sure looks like a big school," said Davy while his mind raced. Should he take this boy now or wait? He wasn't sure. Maybe he should just see if he could talk this boy into going with him.

"Where do you live?" asked Davy.

That question caused a swirl of mixed emotions inside Justin. This guy seemed harmless enough and yet his school had taught him to never answer such questions. He knew he shouldn't stay and talk, especially if the stranger started talking about stuff like where he lived and did he walk here every day and about his parents. He started to turn away, but something held him there. His pain had faded and even his stomach felt better. Still, he knew he should use more caution.

"In a house, right down the street there," he said pointing over his shoulder.

"I live in a special place," Davy told him quietly.

"Where?"

Davy pointed in the air behind the school. "It's in the mountains, there's a huge house built right into a cave. The place is full of kids. They have toys and candy. Nobody ever gets hurt there."

"What kids are there?"

"Kids that get hurt at home. Their parents don't love them and so they go there where people love them and take care of them."

"Who takes care of them?"

"Nice people. I know them. They're really, really nice."

Davy let his mind bring up the image of Protection and the peaceful scene brought a smile to his face. He remembered the sparkle of the two children he had seen there and his face shone with reflected joy. He had almost forgotten that Justin stood there.

Justin didn't have a reply to that. He felt the soft pleasant flow wash over him again and the words this man spoke laid on him like a warm blanket.

Silence filled the space between the two as Davy pictured Protection in his mind and Justin tried to imagine a place where he wouldn't have to be scared or get spanked. A passing car broke the silence.

"I better get to school, mister," said Justin.

Davy thought about standing up, taking the boy's hand and leading him away right then. He looked at the boy and tried again to gage the depth of hurt and size of the black hole. He knew that the boy wasn't quite ready. He decided to give him more time.

"Maybe I'll see you tomorrow," said Davy.

"Sure thing mister," replied Justin.

"My name is Davy," he said, holding out his hand.

Justin looked at it and with his alarm bells silenced, he held out his hand. "Mine's Justin."

They shook hands and then Justin ran across the street. Davy watched him until he disappeared behind the school. He looked up and down the street again and still didn't see any other children. He lifted the paper again and pretended to read some more. When the bus came ten minutes later, he got on.

Justin watched him from the school window trying to regain the feeling that had evaporated as soon as Justin had crossed the street. The pain in his legs and buttocks returned along with his stomach ache. He began think he shouldn't have stopped and talked to the stranger. He continued to watch until he saw the guy named Davy get on the bus. Then he began to walk the hallways, thinking, his mind returning to a place called Protection. He spent most of the day dreaming about that place where no one would hurt him.

Davy sat on the bus and shook uncontrollably. He crossed his legs, afraid he would wet himself. He peeked at the other people on the bus trying to see if they stared at him. He thought that any moment the police would stop the bus and arrest him. He turned to see if there were cop cars with flashing lights following him like he saw on TV. He just knew they would catch him and put him in jail. He wanted to throw up, but that would only make matters worse. He closed his eyes and tried to focus on Protection. He could picture it, the soft lights and comfortable pillows. He could see the smiling faces and the nice Mr. Harrington. That poor boy he met today deserved to go there. It was that thought that settled Davy enough to quit shuddering. He looked up when the bus stopped. He got off without looking at anyone and began walking unsteadily toward work.

***

Unbelievably, Roberta had kept her promise. She hadn't told a soul. She had even remembered everything Davy had shown her. She had done so without writing it down but by forcing herself to think about it non-stop since Davy had left. Her hand went to her cheek where Davy had kissed her. She hadn't forgotten that either.

She really couldn't wait to do her part and hoped that it would come soon. All during the day they had spent together, Davy had been pacing circles around her and fumbling his words. He had seemed different to Roberta but she shrugged it off. He was Davy. He lived on his own. Was there anything he couldn't do? For the first time in their relationship, she hadn't felt like spitting out any smart remarks. She had seen his furrowed brow and knew something troubled him.

***

Justin spent another terrifying night at home made even harder by the conversation he had with the stranger, who wasn't really a stranger after all, now that Justin knew his name. The thought that some place existed where he could go and nobody would ever hurt him again had filled him with a longing. But a nagging idea that his mother would be lonely also pained him. Ghostly memories of good times wafted through him. Her warm lap and soft hugs could not be forgotten. The laughter and games they used to play appeared in his mind as clear as if it were last night. He looked up at his closed door and listened hard for his mother. He heard the bottle hit the glass and knew she was pouring another. He thought that if he ever saw that stranger again, he would ask him how to get to the place. He heard his mother singing to some sad song on the radio, another sign that a new beating was coming soon. He hoped and prayed it wouldn't happen tonight. He froze when he heard the scrape of her chair across the kitchen floor.

TWELVE

"Hi, Roberta," Davy said into the phone.

"Hey, Davy," said Roberta.

"Is there anyone around you right now?" Davy asked.

Roberta looked in both directions. She couldn't see anyone. She heard laughter coming from the entertainment room.

"No, Davy. They're all watching stupid TV."

"Listen, Roberta. Can you get a pass for Saturday?" Davy whispered.

Roberta knew right away that Davy wasn't talking about a walk in the park or another trip to the supermarket.

"I can ask. I've been good and if I tell them I'm going with you, it should be easy," Roberta whispered back.

"You can't tell them you are going with me. You need an alone pass."

"I don't know. They have never given me a pass for just myself. I could just leave. They don't lock the doors. Nobody would know."

"No. That won't work. When they find you missing, they'll call the police. No. You have to get a pass."

"I could ask for a few hours to go pretend shopping."

"Do whatever you can."

"Is it for something special?"

"I can't tell you that. Just get a pass. I'll call you tomorrow night to tell you what we're going to do. I have to go now."

"Okay, I'll wait. Bye."

Davy paced the floor in his apartment. He had been wrong to involve Roberta. She would probably blab it to Mrs. Anderson when she tried to get permission to go out alone. He knew that the cops would come knocking at his door any time. Every sound, every slam of a car door made him jump. He only told her because he had to tell someone or he'd explode. Alternating between worry and anger, he paced the room.

He still questioned the plan; his fear of being caught diminished only by the image of Protection and the happiness within. Then he remembered Justin and the fear and pain he had felt coming from the small boy. He knew he had to do something.

Davy tossed and turned that night as dreams interrupted his sleep, stealing away his comfort and projecting policemen and jail cells into his mind.

The next morning Davy sat at the bus stop waiting for Justin to appear. Again, he hid behind a newspaper as he scanned the block for people watching. The paper he held shook too much to read, but Davy didn't read very well, anyway.

"Hey Davy!"

Davy's turmoil was so intense that he didn't even feel Justin approach. He jumped and turned quickly at the voice that came over his shoulder. He saw Justin flinch at his sudden movement. Davy also felt a small stab of pain flow from Justin as he reacted in fear to the unexpected response from Davy. Davy quickly sent a tickle into Justin to calm him and then put on his biggest smile.

"Hello, Justin," said Davy. "You surprised me." Then Davy held out his hand.

Justin walked over and took it. They shook hands and Justin smiled.

"How are you today?" Davy said.

"Okay, I guess. No school tomorrow."

"What're you going to do? Play at the playground?"

"Hey, Davy," started Justin quietly. "Can anyone go to that place you told me about?"

"Protection?" Davy looked around checking for people nearby. "Not everyone. Just kids that are hurt and me and Mr. Harrington."

Davy slapped his hand over his mouth. He wasn't supposed to tell about Mr. Harrington. He looked at Justin, worried that he may know him and here, Davy had let out the secret. Justin didn't seem to notice.

"How do you get there? Is it far?"

"It's not too far. In fact I want to go tomorrow. I suppose you could follow along."

"Well my mom says I can't leave the block, but she doesn't really watch. You don't steal children do you? My mom always says to not go with strangers 'cause they steal kids and hurt them."

"Your mom's right about strangers, I learned the same thing when I was little, but I'm not a stranger am I? Besides, I haven't asked you to come. I said you can tag along. That means you can come and go whenever you want. But I'm going tomorrow if you want to see the place."

"What time are you going? To Protection. That's a funny name you know."

"Tomorrow, early. If you want, meet me here at 8 a.m. I might have a friend with me. A girl."

"I guess that's all right. Maybe I'll see you tomorrow."

Justin ran across the street without looking back. Davy lifted his paper again and waited for the bus, knees pressed tightly together.

***

Davy spent his day in a fog at work. Images swirled through his head and emotions pounded his heart like waves in a hurricane. He found himself stacking beans among the canned milk and cereal in the flour section. Mr. Harrington called him twice to point out the mistakes and had to remind him to go to lunch. He acted so different from his normal self, Mr. Harrington considered sending him home or calling Mrs. Anderson. Davy tried to concentrate harder but he couldn't. Justin, the cave, Roberta, the police, and the children at Protection, all kept up their attack, keeping him from focusing on the present.

***

Mrs. Anderson started to think some strange virus had infected the house. A few nights ago, Davy had been distant and distracted during the Independent Living Classes and now Roberta acted out of character. She had come to see her twice about an unescorted pass for Saturday. The first time she refused, Roberta had burst into tears and had run to her room. Mrs. Anderson didn't think Roberta would be safe outside the home on her own and, in fact, felt she may never be. Her memory was the problem. She forgot things moments after they occurred. Sometimes she even forgot her room number. Mrs. Anderson hadn't worried about the outburst because she knew Roberta would forget about it before she got down the hall. Then Roberta came back and asked for a day pass again. Mrs. Anderson opened her mouth to tell her that they had already discussed it when Roberta stopped her.

"I know you already said no and I shouldn't have run away crying. I just wanted to practice being independent and it means so much to me."

Mrs. Anderson sat back in her chair. Roberta had remembered, she thought to herself. How strange.

"Roberta, you know I can't let you. You're not ready. What if you get lost and can't find your way home?"

"I can find my way home. It's just down the street to the supermarket."

"I'm sorry honey, I just can't. I can let you go in a group or with Davy for a little bit, but not alone."

"No! I mean no. I want to go alone."

"Why alone?"

"Because. Because … well, I need to."

Roberta wanted to tell her about her important mission. She wanted to tell her that Davy would make sure she got home. She wanted to tell her that she was being a stupid housemother. Roberta felt a hot spark in the center of her forehead and she wanted to send it rifling into Mrs. Anderson, but she held back. She gripped the edge of the table instead. She was able to deflect her anger knowing it would only lead to trouble and Mrs. Anderson had always been nice. It seemed important. She looked up and saw Mrs. Anderson with a genuine smile on her face. Mrs. Anderson got up and came around the desk to where Roberta sat. She shocked her by bending down and giving her a hug. Hugs weren't common in the house.

"I'm really impressed and proud of you," she said. "You remembered our first talk and now you took no without a tantrum. You are growing up and I wouldn't be surprised if you could get your own day pass soon."

Roberta sensed an opening and almost asked again, but instead she stayed quiet. She hugged Mrs. Anderson and walked back to her room, trying to think of another way. Roberta made a promise to herself; she wouldn't let Davy down.

***

Justin shook his head and looked at the teacher. He saw his mouth move but didn't hear the words. He was daydreaming to his own image of Protection. He spent most of the day there playing with toys he imagined and seeing the smiling Davy with the big soft eyes. He hung on to the wonderful feelings that appeared out of nowhere. He even had to spend a few minutes in time out earlier when he didn't answer when called on. He didn't mind because he couldn't get in trouble for not paying attention while he stood in the corner. Things changed when the bell rang and children raced out of the school to go home. Justin stood on the steps of the school facing the busses and watched as mothers picked up their children. He saw them hugging and kissing, happy parents and happy children. Justin looked for his mother, wishing, more than believing, she would be there. She used to come and get him. He would see her sitting in the car and she would smile and wave to him. They would sometimes go to McDonald's for fries before going home or to the park to play. At night, she would sit close enough to feel the softness of her skin against his arm, and go over his schoolwork with him. She would give him hugs and kisses when he got the answers right. He reached up and wiped his eyes with the back of his hand.

Today, like the last few months, his mother didn't show. He could picture her sitting at home, in the kitchen, maybe already waiting for him. Justin looked around for Davy. Maybe Davy decided to go to Protection early and he could go with him now. Justin reached behind and felt the lump on his back that had just started to go down. It hurt to touch it. He could feel his bruises on the bones under his butt where it always hurt to sit. Somehow he knew another beating approached, maybe tonight. Protection would come a day too late. Dread filled Justin as he began his slow plodding walk home. As he made his way up the block, he stopped at every opportunity. He checked out the bugs that crawled across his path or re-tied his shoelaces. He considered running away right then. He could hide out until tomorrow, but knew his mother would have police combing the area. She wouldn't be cheated out of her revenge. Maybe it wouldn't be tonight, he tried unsuccessfully to tell himself. Maybe she would be asleep already, maybe dead. That thought struck Justin hard. He loved his mother in spite of the beatings. She couldn't help it. His dad had left and it was Justin's fault. His dad had called him a little termite, one that ate through paychecks. He looked up and saw his house. Why did the walk home always seem so short? The house sat there dark and foreboding, back from the street, hidden behind trees. He turned up the sidewalk, one foot in front of the other, like the condemned to the gallows. When he reached the bottom step he heard his mother bellow.

"Justin!"

THIRTEEN

Davy nervously paced around his apartment. Earlier, he had tried watching television, but found his mind walking the trail to Protection. He looked at the floor as he moved and wondered how much longer until he would see a path worn into the carpeting. He suspected he had walked in circles long enough to equal the distance he would travel tomorrow.

He tried to review his plan, but realized it wasn't really a plan; snatch and run like all the police shows talked about. He would get Justin and go as fast as he could, hoping to reach Protection before anyone noticed Justin missing.

Now he wasn't sure why he had asked Roberta to help or why he wanted her to go along with him. At first he just wanted to tell someone before the secret burst and she was the only one he thought he could tell. He thought she would forget as she always did. But not this time. He just knew she would blab to someone about the pass and then everything would be messed up. Why he suggested she go with him, he didn't know. She would surly slow him down. Then again, could she even hike the distance to Protection? Maybe he should just go to the school and not stop at the house. If he did that, she may get mad and then tell. It was all so confusing. She probably wouldn't get a pass anyway, he thought, not knowing if it made him happy or sad.

He had called her earlier to find out if she had told anyone. He tried to joke with her, but she didn't respond. She had sounded different, not as talkative as usual and she had called him Davy, not dumb old stock boy. He wondered if she had remembered the pass. She didn't mention it, so he decided to let it drop in case people were close to her and could overhear. Again, he didn't understand the differences in his feelings, happy, sad, excited, and scared all at the same time. He ended the call by telling her he hoped to see her early tomorrow, about seven. All she had said was, "Okay." Davy stood there looking at the phone for a long time, unsure of what any of it meant.

He looked out his window toward the cave, toward Protection. He wondered if Mr. Harrington sat on the couch with the two children, waiting for him. Night had come and hid the mountains, but Davy knew the direction of Protection. His face showed in the reflection from the window and his big round eyes stared back. For the first time he saw his face without a smile and it depressed him even more. He turned from the window and looked around his apartment. He had never felt so scared or so alone as he did now. He should be happy now that he had responsibility and he should be proud he had been selected to help someone. Yet, he felt a weight, like a heavy blanket pressing down on his shoulders. He dropped back into his chair and watched the flickering television without really seeing it.

***

When Justin walked through the door from school, his mother was in her usual place at the kitchen table. Stacks of paper were piled on it and her glass sat next to a half bottle of clear liquid. Maybe an old bottle, he thought, one that had been half full when she started on it, but he couldn't lie to himself. She already looked half drunk. He entered the kitchen stiff legged and frightened.

"Where've you been!" she asked

Justin knew that tone. It started to change with the first drink and got progressively worse.

When his dad had first left it hadn't been too bad. They had gotten on like two chums. Even then she drank, but not as much and after a few drinks, she would turn up the radio and dance with him. That had all changed now.

"School," he replied quietly.

His mother looked up at the clock. Justin watched as she squinted to see the time and knew by that action the bottle had been full only a short time ago. He coiled himself to run. If she made any move toward him, Justin knew he would run out the door as fast as he could. Instead, she looked back at him. He saw the look, unfocused, one eye peering intently, another of the signals he had learned to read. She stared at him like some kind of awful insect.

"You're late. Where have you been? Never mind, I'll deal with that later. Go to your room and do your homework."

Justin briefly looked at the refrigerator, wondering if he dared to open it and grab a snack. His stomach growled and he wanted a drink. In the end, his hurts whispered to him and he walked quickly out of the kitchen. Later, he thought, when she falls asleep, knowing it was a lie.

Justin sat in his room writing out his spelling words, slowly and neatly. He thought if he could do them perfectly, his mother might smile and muss his hair like she used to. He looked up startled and cringed when he heard a loud crash in the kitchen. His eyes darted everywhere in panic, looking for a hiding spot and then to the door, expecting to see his mother come storming through. Moments passed without further sound. Justin got up from his little desk and crept to his door. He cracked it open and listened. He could hear his mother in the kitchen talking to herself; every other word a bad one. He closed the door softly and tiptoed to his dresser. Having made his decision, he immediately felt better. He pulled out some clothes, a few things to wear tomorrow and stuffed them in his school bag. He quietly opened his window. The chilled night air flowed in and he shivered. He dropped the bag outside to the ground. He would take it with him in the morning when he went to meet Davy and make the trip to Protection. His stomach rolled and he looked back in the general direction of the kitchen. He knew he wouldn't go out there tonight. He had seen his mother like this only once before and she had hurt him badly. Just thinking about it woke old bruises.

He thought about leaving right then, following his bag out the window, but instead, pictured his mother, sitting all alone in the kitchen, crying. He couldn't stop loving her even in the face of what she may do. His own tears, squeezed out in frustration, came. Then he began to cuss like her, quietly. He cursed at his missing father, the liquor she drank, and at God for making her sad. He even saved a few choice words for himself because if he hadn't been such a termite, maybe things would still be okay. He found himself crying at the hopelessness of his situation. He laid his head on his arms, chest hitching back the last of his tears, crying himself to sleep.

***

Roberta sat on her bed with her hands folded in her lap. She had her pajamas and slippers on. She looked at the crumpled paper in her hand. She had written 'get a pass' on it and she remembered that Mrs. Anderson hadn't given her one. Now she had to remember why she wanted one. Whatever the reason, if it had to do with Davy, she'd get one.

She waited for the staff to turn out the lights and start their nightly bed check of all the residents. She knew that sometime later they would go into the staff bedroom and go to sleep. Then she would sneak down and take one from the office. She could forge a name and maybe get Mr. B, the weekend person, to let her go. Mrs. Anderson had already left and wouldn't return until Monday.

She crossed her room and opened her door a crack to see if everyone had gone to bed. She could hear the voices from the other group members still echoing up and down the hall. She looked at the digital clock beside her bed. Above it, on a piece of cardboard, she could see all the important times written. One had a big 10:00, which was bedtime for the house. Her clock showed 9:22. She lay down on her bed to wait. Her eyes slowly closed as she tried to imagine the next day. What did Davy want?

She woke with a start and lay there looking at the ceiling. Wisps of her dream began to break apart like fog on a sunny morning. She tried to hold on to them, but they slipped between her fingers as she tried to snatch them from the air. She captured one thing, an image of her mother. It made her feel safe and warm, like when she curled up on her mother's lap so many years ago. Then, she had felt real comfort and love. She stayed on her back clutching her hands to her chest, holding her mother's image tight. It began to evaporate. Roberta tried even harder to hold on to the feeling. Tears began to build up in her eyes as the frustration filled her. Anger at her inability to hold a thought filled the void left by her dream. She opened her eyes. Her eyes narrowed on the clock and its staring red numbers. It tumbled end over end and landed on the carpet by her door. Roberta lay still with the numbers from the clock burned into her mind; 1:00. She looked at the now dark clock on the floor by her door. She noticed her hand was balled into a fist. She opened it under the light from her desk lamp and looked at the paper she held, crushed and damp. 'Get a pass' it read. It had something to do with Davy.

She got up off her bed and tiptoed to her door. She brushed the clock aside with her foot as she wondered how it had got there. Again, she put her ear to the door and listened. Not a sound came to her. She turned the knob and slowly opened it, expecting Mr. B to be standing there. Mr. B had too many letters in his name. Nobody in the house could say his name right so they called him Mr. B. He was old and smiled a lot. He stayed in the home on weekends and after dark. She stood in the doorway and didn't know why. She looked at her hand again. The day pass! She saw the light spill out from her room so she turned off the switch. For a moment, everything went black. Slowly, her eyes adjusted and she could see the light from the little plug-in things that glowed along the length of the hall. She slipped out of her room and closed her door. She turned and looked up at it. She read the number, 7, as she always did. Then she walked quietly down the hall toward the office.

**

An explosion woke Justin up and a current of fear ripped through his body. Out of habit, he began to move. She had surprised him and the first blow slammed into his butt before he could deflect it. He moved to dodge the next blow and the wood handle slammed into his lower back. His eyes squeezed shut and pinpricks of light flashed behind his eyelids, as he momentarily curled into a ball. He didn't wait for the next one to land. He rolled hard away from the rampaging, screaming, demon in his room. The next blow came to his hip as he turned to escape. The grazing blow didn't hurt as much but he still winced. He could barely make out the slurred words screaming from his mother's mouth.

"Youlittlesonofabitchofanogoodfather. Getoutherenow!"

Justin looked up from his temporary haven. His mother couldn't reach him from the other side of the bed. He barely recognized her with her face twisted into a drunken snarl. She looked like the dog down the street, the pit bull behind the fence. It would bark, growl, and snap its teeth while drool flew everywhere. Everyone knew the dog would kill if it got loose and now he saw the same thing in his mother. His earlier sadness at leaving vanished, tossed out without so much as a thought. Escaping this rabid animal that had taken over his mother became his only goal.

She leapt across the bed, broom handle raised. He hadn't been expecting such a move and froze as the wild figure flew at him. At the last moment, he ducked, but this time he moved too slow and again bright sparkles of light appeared as the weapon crashed against the side of his head. She had never hit him there before. His room went gray and for a moment the silly thought that it had become foggy crossed his mind. His position wedged the bed away from the wall, spilling him to the floor, stunned.

His mother lay fully stretched out across the bed and she, too, had gone strangely silent. She saw the lump already building on the side of his head and a trickle of blood running down to his neck. Justin recovered first and rolled under the bed. His mother came back alive after that.

"It's your own fault! If you just hold still this will all be over in a minute."

Justin paused for just a second when he heard her voice drop. It had gone suddenly normal. No screaming. That was worse. It was terrifying. He stayed right in the middle of the floor under the bed. He looked to see where she was so he could move away. It was difficult to focus. He expected the mattress to fly off at any second. He looked down and saw two drops of blood splatter on the floor. He closed one eye and saw only one drop. Reaching up, he touched the side of his head. He could feel the lump. It felt the size of a baseball and his hand came away wet with blood.

The bed above him began to protest and he knew his mother crawled across the top. She had started to coo at him, trying to entice him out but he wasn't fooled. The bend in the springs gave away her location. Her voice sounded deeper and he picked up an undertone he had not heard before. He followed the bulging springs gauging which direction she moved. He could sometimes see her feet along the edge, although through his crossed eyes, he would see four instead of two. She got off the bed and staggered backward. He watched her feet from his position in the center. They worked down on the side of the bed, then to the foot. He could see her taking small steps to steady herself. She tried to circle around behind, trying to trap him. Without thinking, without knowing why, Justin reached out and grabbed an ankle with each hand and held on tight. Her first attempt to kick his hands free caused her to lose balance. Justin could feel her going and he slid further under the bed, pulling her ankles with him. The floor shook when she landed. Justin could see her face as she rolled to her side and looked at him. He saw hate coming from narrow eyes. He moved quickly now, coming out from under the bed. He jumped to his feet, but found his knees wouldn't lock. Then he too, fell to the floor, his head just missing the dresser. He heard his bed sliding across the floor behind him as his mother pushed it away from her. He didn't turn to confirm what he already knew. She had gone completely silent and this scared him more than the screaming, more than the cooing. He crawled to the doorway on his hands and knees. Her hand grabbed his foot but he pulled it away before her grip tightened. He pushed himself back to his feet and staggered down the hall. Even in his panicked state, the sight of the refrigerator woke his stomach. He wanted to pause and grab something from inside but he heard his mother trying to get up, trashing his room as she did. Justin fled the house into the dark of night. He took a hard right feeling the gravel under his sneakers scratch across the concrete sidewalk. At the edge of the house he took another hard turn to get around the corner of the house and out of his mother's sight. He stopped at the side and listened, wondering if she would follow him outside.

"Justin!"

He cringed but the sound came from inside so he held his ground.

"Justin!"

This time it blasted out through the kitchen door. Was she coming? He stayed still, waiting for her to make the next move. He looked at both corners of the house wondering if she would try to sneak up from behind.

He turned quickly when the shade on the window right beside him flew open and light poured out. Justin turned to see his mother, her face hidden behind a mask of rage, and the broomstick coming like a baseball bat. He froze as his heart leapt to his throat.

"Justin!"

He ran as he heard the window smash behind him, the voice of his mother drowning out all other sounds, following him down the alley.

"Justin! Come back here right now!"

He ran as fast and as far as he could, twisting his way between houses and crossing backyards. He finally stopped when he reached familiar territory, the back of the school. He edged around the corner, hoping for a miracle, that Davy would be at the bus stop already. The area looked as dark and deserted as the rest of the street. Justin walked back to the rear of the school and squeezed in-between the big air conditioner units. He would be safe there, he thought. As he sat feeling the residual warmth of the tin, he worried that his mother would call the police to search for him. If they found him, they would take him back home. Nervous, he got up from his hiding spot. A wave of dizziness almost sent him crashing back to the ground. When the spell passed, he went around to the side of the building again to check for the police cars he knew he would see, lights flashing, coming to take him home.

***

Davy looked out the window then down at his feet. He turned his thoughts to Justin, recalling the black hole inside of the boy. Davy couldn't imagine the pain and fear that filled the boy. That thought helped strengthen his determination. As he paced around on the carpet, a thought came to him. He wondered if he could touch him from here. He had never tried, never thought to. He didn't understand how his special talent worked. He only knew it worked by looking into their eyes and picturing a shower of tickles entering through them. As for Justin, he only knew the general direction, somewhere toward the school. Even though Justin was probably asleep in bed, Davy wanted to try to reach him. He placed his chin in his palms and faced toward the school. He pictured Justin and then squeezed hard, pouring the feeling into the thought, imagining it traveling through the air like a happy wind.

***

Justin decided it would be safer to keep moving through the night. He wandered the streets, never going more than four blocks from the school. Soon, the cool of the evening dew began to stick to him. He remembered his school bag and the warm clothes inside. He imagined sneaking back and retrieving it until the memory of his mother's face in the window returned. He didn't dare go back there, no matter how cold or hungry he got. After what seemed like hours, he noticed that most of the lights in the houses that lined the streets had gone off. Very few cars drove through the neighborhood and when one did, he hid in the bushes. When he couldn't walk any more, he found a thick hedge and crawled inside. Just before a restless sleep claimed him, a warm peaceful feeling swept through him like it did when he saw Davy and the word Protection whispered through his chest.

FOURTEEN

Roberta snuck down the hall pausing every few seconds to listen. She could hear the refrigerator running and saw the soft light coming from the kitchen nightlights, spaced every few outlets. The entrance to the kitchen was on her left. She moved past it, glancing inside to make sure there wasn't anyone in there. She saw the bright white of the stove and refrigerator reflecting the shine from the little bulbs covered by plastic. She felt her heart beating quicker than normal and she was so tense her muscles ached. She looked wildly around; kitchen, hall, living room ahead. What was she doing out here in the middle of the night? Suddenly she couldn't remember.

She felt her fingernails biting into her palm. She lifted her hand into the reflected brightness from the kitchen. Crumpled inside her hand, sat a piece of paper, soft from the sweat of her palm. She opened it carefully and looked at it. Now she remembered. She put the paper in her other hand and continued her journey down the hall, freezing for just a moment and stifling a scream when she heard the squeak of a door opening behind her. Roberta tiptoed quickly into the large living room and sat on the couch. She bent over as far as she could and held her knees. No light shined in there, no little bulbs plugged into the wall sockets gave her light. She heard footsteps coming in her direction. She pulled herself into a tighter ball and tears began to form in her eyes as fear of being caught began to overwhelm her. She expected the light to come on at any moment and a hand to grab her shoulder. Roberta held her breath, huddled there, not moving, waiting for the end. She heard another door open and close. Her nose starting running and drops of tears wet her leg as she trembled on the couch. The flushing toilet made the next sound. It roared in the silent house. She almost jumped up and ran before she recognized it. She could place the squeak of the hinges as the bathroom door opened and closed again. After a moment, she heard another door shut with an audible click. She listened until the water in the toilet stopped running. Slowly, she sat up, nervously looking over her shoulder almost expecting to see someone standing there looking at her.

Carefully, on shaky knees, she stood and again waited, listening for footsteps. She eased over to the corner and peeked down the hall. When she saw the empty hallway, she relaxed a bit and looked around as if for the first time. Why was she sitting in the living room in the dark? Again, she felt, more than saw, her one hand balled into a fist. This time the memory returned before she opened it. She wiped the nervous sweat from her forehead. At the end of the hall, past the kitchen, past the living room, an old bedroom had been turned into the house office. Roberta continued in that direction. Standing in front of the office door, she reached out and grabbed the knob. It twisted in her hand but wouldn't open. Locked. There she stood; one hand on the knob, one holding the paper, sweat re-forming on her forehead, eyes filled with tears, heart beating way too fast. Roberta didn't know how long she stood there, but she knew it was too long. She could see all the way down the hall, back toward the bedrooms. If anyone came out now, they couldn't miss her standing where she shouldn't be. She thought of Betty and how she would laugh and tease her for being at the wrong door. Then she thought of Mrs. Anderson who wouldn't give her a pass. The anger began to build, anger toward Betty and Mrs. Anderson, but mostly at herself and how she couldn't remember. She could imagine everyone laughing at her, even the door that wouldn't open. She stared at it with fire in her eyes. Open! The door gave way with a crack. It swung open on its own. Roberta stared at it as it finished its arc. Then she walked in.

She stood still as she looked around the dark room, no light to guide her. She flipped on the light switch over by the doorframe, flooding the room with a sudden brilliance causing her to squint. She felt tears pool in her eyes, then run down her cheeks, following the trail etched there by the earlier ones. She used her clenched fist to brush them away then pushed the door shut from the inside, giving it a warning look that said I dare you to lock again. She looked around the room as if seeing it for the first time. The fear, momentarily erased by the anger, returned. She walked around the desk and with a shaky hand pulled open the top drawer. Just pens and pencils rolled around. She looked up at the door before looking in the next drawer. A yellow square pad of passes had to be in one of them. She opened the other drawers looking for the familiar passbook. There it was, in the top left drawer. She pulled the pad out and set it on the desk looking at the blanks, wondering how to fill them in. She didn't know much about time or days or how to write cursive well enough to mimic Mrs. Anderson's handwriting. She picked up a pencil but her hand shook badly. She pulled several off the pad anyway and put it back in the drawer. As she left the office, she saw several splinters scattered about on the floor and saw where the wood had cracked by the lock. How did that happen, she wondered? She turned off the light and almost in a daze she went back to her room, checking the number on the door several times to make sure she had the right one.

She set the blank passes on her desk without another thought and dropped the crumpled ball of paper from her fist right beside them. She felt exhausted and flopped back on her bed, passes, Davy, and her appointment tomorrow forgotten.

***

Davy's eyes snapped open. He didn't move. The last twenty-four hours swept through him with a new clarity as he rolled his head toward the mountain and closed his eyes to visualize Protection. This time the image came disjointed. He couldn't see the children or Mr. Harrington; he couldn't even remember the smile the children had worn. He opened his eyes again, frightened by his lack of ability to remember the scene. That made him think of Roberta and how easily she forgot things. Was it happening to him? That thought frightened him even more. Darkness filled his bedroom with only a faint glow from the bathroom nightlight. The clock showed five a.m. He sat up and turned on the lamp beside his bed filling the room with its brilliance. Beside him, on the nightstand, lay his schedule, written in his familiar scribble. Get up at 6:00, shower, eat, brush teeth, Monday, Wednesday, Friday get ready for work. Tuesday, Thursday set alarm for noon to get ready for work. Davy had these notes all over his apartment to remember to do important things. He ran his finger down the list reading the items one by one. A chill went through him as he realized for the first time in his life, that none of them really applied to him today. No more lists. Today he became a man with responsibility. He had a new job; to take a child to Protection. Davy wondered why he felt so bad for doing something so good. His thoughts turned to Justin. He wondered what Justin was doing. Had he woken up yet? Had he dressed for the trip? He recalled the look in the boy's eyes; sad, scared, and excited. Davy also remembered the pain and blackness he sensed inside Justin, the worst he had ever felt. The anguish sat deep and layered, physical and emotional. He shuddered involuntarily at the thought of the incredible pain that Justin must have endured to be filled with such agony. Davy pulled up his belt and decided to put away his fears, Justin needed his help. With his momentary dread pushed aside, replaced with anger at the source of that abuse, he walked into his bathroom, ready to follow the daily list until he left his apartment.

He looked in the mirror and saw a big round white face with big funny eyes and straight black hair. He hated and loved his eyes. They set him apart from the normal adults, but they brought the children joy.

Well, his eyes didn't separate him from all the adults. There was Roberta. He wondered if she got the pass or if she even remembered. He would go by the house on his way to the bus stop just to see if she did, not really expecting her. Even with her memory and moodiness, Davy longed for company on this trip. He began his routine, maybe for the last time.

***

Roberta fought the alarm. In her dreams, she stood in Mrs. Anderson's office with her hand in the drawer, trying to steal passes. The alarm on the wall blared. She could hear people coming to investigate and she could hear Mrs. Anderson yelling down the hall.

"What's going on down there? Who's in my office? It'll be back to the foster home for whoever's in there!"

Roberta pulled and pulled, trying to get her hand out. It didn't hurt but it wouldn't come loose either. She leaned back hard, using all her weight and it popped out. She lost her balance and began falling backwards.

She woke with a start when she hit the floor beside her bed. She wasn't hurt, but it surprised her. She didn't get up off the floor right away as she struggled between the dream and reality. She had a difficult time separating the two. Her confusion held her captive and she began to cry. She slowly became aware of people running down the hall, apparently coming to see what caused the noise, Mr. B's voice the loudest of all, shouting for the others to get out of the way. Roberta's eyes caught the bright yellow paper on her desk. She moved quickly now, still frightened by the dream, but sure she had to hide the passes. She swept them into the desk drawer the same time the door opened. Mr. B stood there with his eyes wide and staring.

"What happened? You okay? Are you hurt?" Mr. B asked, his eyes swept the room.

Other voices, mixed together, also streamed into the room.

"What's going on? I can't see! Where's Roberta? Is it a robber?"

Mr. B turned sharply and scowled at the other residents behind him and they quieted. He turned back toward Roberta who sat on her bed.

"I'm alright Mr. B. I just had a dream. I fell out of bed."

"You sure?"

Roberta could see him peering at her now with one scrunched eye.

"Yes, Mr. B. I'm fine now," she said as she wiped away the tears.

"Okay, time to get up anyway."

He turned and again scowled at the group gathered outside her door. The group broke up and started back to their rooms, Betty last, giving Roberta a smirk.

Roberta didn't even respond. She had enough trouble just talking to Mr. B. She had been chanting the word 'passes' silently to herself as he had asked questions. It had been very difficult to formulate answers as she continued to repeat the word in her head. She didn't want to forget it. Passes. She had to remember them because they were important. She had something to do today and it had to do with passes. After Mr. B left her alone again, she looked back at her desk and saw a crumpled piece of paper there. She picked it up and unfolded it. She read the words scribbled in her own handwriting. She laid it back on her dresser and went to the shower to get ready for the day. She had an appointment.

Roberta returned from the shower and her eyes went right to the note. She sat at her desk and slid the drawer open. She stared at the passes, wondering where they had come from and why they lay there in her desk. Again, she looked at the crumpled note. She laid it on the desk and smoothed it with her hand. 'Get a pass.' She knew what it meant and she obviously had, but why? She put the two blank passes beside the wrinkled paper and stared at them as she got dressed. She didn't know how to call the memory back. She clenched her jaw and began pushing with her mind. She stopped even before she could start. The fleeting memory of breaking in to the office shocked her. She wanted to remember. She tried rapping her knuckles against her head, first softly and then a bit harder, until it hurt. Nothing. She looked at her clock, almost eight, time to eat. She started to walk out of the room and then stopped. She turned and went back to her desk. She looked down at the passes and the note again. She opened her drawer and put the yellow slips of paper back inside where they would be out of sight. She closed it and walked out without the paper in her hand. She could smell the food in the kitchen and she hurried down the hall.

***

Davy stood at his front door staring into space. He paused to mentally run down a new list, one not written anywhere. He dangled his hiking bag from his hand, the very thing he was thinking about. He had water, a whole bunch of snacks, bus fare for two, and two flashlights. He went back to his room for more money, sure that Roberta wouldn't have any, and then back to the refrigerator to pick out some stuff for Roberta to eat, just in case. He grabbed a prepackaged lunch, the ones he normally packed for work. Work. Would he ever go back there? He had thought more than once that he would just stay at Protection. He could go into the city and find abused children there and return with them to Protection every night. Maybe he would.

He paused once more. He went through his list again. He could picture it pretty good. He had printed it in his mind in big red crayon. He felt his front pocket and pulled out the index card. In the center he had drawn a large black circle. Davy shuddered as the color emitted a chill that ran right through his center. It reminded him of what he felt in the closet as a child. He quickly slid it back into his pocket. Now he reached out and put his finger on the list posted by his door; lights off, water off, stove off, TV off, keys in pocket. He tapped his pocket and felt them there. He opened the door and stepped out into the hall. He looked back inside once more before closing the door. He felt his home would never be the same again.

***

Justin peered out from his hiding spot inside the hedge. He could see the bench at the bus stop in the growing morning light. He clasped his arms around himself against the cold damp air. He felt dizzy and his stomach rolled. The short stiff branches of the hedge stabbed into him from every direction, scratching his neck and arms. He reached up and carefully probed the lump on his head. It felt soft and tender. When he touched it a thin electric bolt of pain shot from the center to his feet. A trail of dried blood from the lump ran through his hair down to his neck. His collar was stiff from it. The bruise in his back throbbed and when he twisted to make his position more comfortable, a needle of pain would race to his stomach. He clenched his teeth to keep from throwing up. He huddled into a ball trying to get warm. The hedge had not kept the chill of the high mountain air off of him, the cold made him shiver. As he held himself, he thought of his warm bed at home and the refrigerator full of food. He tried to think of a way he could return. Could he sneak past his mother who should be sleeping at the kitchen table? He thought of his school bag outside his window and the warm clothes in it. He carefully squirmed his way out of his hiding spot. Another pain shot through him, and with it a refreshed memory of the beating he took last night. What if she's awake? What if he wakes her? She would finish the job. There would be no going home. Still, he couldn't stay in the bushes any longer;

he had to get moving. He looked around at the still dark houses and the empty streets.

He stood on the sidewalk in pain. His body didn't want to straighten out. It protested all the way from his back to his head. His eyes wouldn't focus and his feet didn't want to obey. Staggering like a drunk, he worked his way to the back of the school again. He returned to the big maze of ductwork that housed the giant heating and air conditioning unit at the rear of the building. The metal felt warm from the running motors. He found a place where he could squeeze between it and the wall. The heat came like an answer to a prayer. As soon as he sat, he went to sleep.

***

The cold mountain air billowing slowly in from the broken window caused Justin's mother to wake up. Her eyes opened to a blur of white from the ceiling. It wasn't the blue from her bedroom or textured like the kitchen. She realized she was in Justin's room, on the floor between the bed and wall. She had stayed there last night waiting for him to come home. She had known she couldn't find him in the dark, but now she couldn't let him be seen by anyone either, although she couldn't quite remember why. She sat up slowly hoping to see him in bed sleeping. When she saw the empty bed, she stood and walked to the kitchen, staggering into the wall several times. She went to the sink and began the task of filling the coffee pot. Once she had it started, she sat at the table. The bills stacked there still stared back at her. With a sweep of her arm they scattered and fell to the floor. She looked at the half bottle of vodka sitting in the center of the table. She reached a shaking hand out and grabbed it. It took both to steady it enough to take a drink. At first she felt it try to come back up. She gritted her teeth and held it down. She could feel the burn and then suddenly, the fire in the pit of her stomach flowed through her like warm sunshine. Her shaking hands settled a bit and her mind cleared. One more sip, she thought. Then I'll be able to think.

She drank a cup of coffee, wincing at the terrible mixture it made in her stomach. She wanted another shot to quiet her raging head, but it nagged her, teased her with a thought that wasn't clear, something about Justin. He wasn't home. He had abandoned her like his father. She put on her jacket and slipped the short broomstick up her sleeve. She left the house and stood where the sidewalk met the street. She would have to find him before anyone else did. Then she would have to bring him home. She had unfinished business. He ran when he should have stayed and helped. She shook her head. She had been thinking of her ex. But Justin ran too. She stood in the early morning light trying to think where he would go. First things first. Keep it simple. Think, think, think. She repeated the sayings she had learned at AA six months ago during her first attempt to quit drinking. Bunch of too happy assholes for people doomed to never drink again, she thought. At least the mantras were good for something, she told herself. She walked around the house checking the bushes and the abandoned doghouse. She found his school bag. He probably went to the school. It was the only other place he knew. She left her yard and walked down the sidewalk toward the school, making the same trip Justin did every day. Every step she took brought her closer to that dirty son of a bitch that would try to abandon her. He belonged to her and that was something the bastard of an ex wasn't going to get, ever!

FIFTEEN

Davy stood outside the group home at the end of the sidewalk. The sun still stayed hidden behind the mountains that rose steeply east of the city. He looked west to the towering buildings of the city center and to the mountains beyond. He turned back to the house and debated whether he should knock. The sidewalk that ran in front and the street remained empty at this time of day. He thought about turning around and walking away without her. They would all be in the kitchen eating breakfast or making their beds. His watch said he had the time it took for the long hand to get to the top before he was supposed to meet Justin. It was at the bottom now. Whatever he decided, he better do it quick.

***

Inside, Roberta had dressed and sat staring at the passes in the drawer of her dresser. The unsigned passes just sat there and she didn't know how she got them. She read the crumpled paper beside them. 'Get passes' it said in her scrawling handwriting. Well, here they sat. Now what? She picked them up and left her room. She wanted to show them to Mr. B and ask him if he knew why she had them.

Roberta saw Mr. B down the hall standing in front of the door to the office, holding the knob, slowly opening and closing the door. Roberta wondered why he didn't go in. He just opened it and closed it with a frown on his face. About half way down the hall, she casually glanced out the window by the front door. Davy! He stood outside on the walk. Without thinking, Roberta turned and went out the door to greet him. Davy saw the bright yellow color of the passes in her hand and his surprise quickly turned to joy. Certainly Roberta must be doing better than he thought if they had given her a pass.

"Roberta! You got the pass!"

Roberta looked down at her hand. "Oh, yeah," she said and held them up.

"Let's go!" Davy said and started walking down the sidewalk to the bus stop.

"Okay," she said and ran to catch up with him.

Roberta had no idea what Davy meant when he said 'let's go', but she trusted him so she walked beside him down the street.

"We have to hurry. Justin's waiting," Davy said.

"Who's Justin?" Roberta asked.

"He's a boy I met. He's one of the ones I have to help. I'll tell you more later, but right now we have to hurry."

Davy walked so fast that Roberta couldn't catch her breath to ask any more questions. She knew that she could get in big trouble for leaving the house without permission. She shrugged it off. She was with Davy so it must be okay, she thought.

***

Mr. B stood looking at the office door for fifteen minutes. First he tried to remember what it looked like when he came on last night. Did they break it during the day and forget to tell him? Did they tell him and he didn't remember? Had he even been in the office since he came on? Certainly it would have been important enough for them to tell him. Then he noticed the splinters on the floor. Surely they would have cleaned them up. He tried to think why anyone would force it open anyway. There really wasn't anything in the office. No money, no stuff worth stealing. He looked around and didn't see anything out of place. Maybe one of the kids had done it mistaking it for their room. They were always forgetting. Accident? Maybe they ran into it while chasing each other. They could get pretty rambunctious. Bah! No sense in playing Dick Tracy. He'd ask them. Mr. B walked up and down the hall asking each one he found, some in the kitchen, some in their rooms. Those he couldn't find, he figured were in the bathroom. Of course nobody knew anything. Now who hadn't he asked? Betty, and there she was, just coming out of the shower, still dressed in her big pink terry cloth robe, matching slippers, and a towel wrapped on her head. He hadn't asked Roberta either.

"Betty, you know anything about the door to the office being broken?"

"No, Mr. B. Who broke it?"

"I don't know. That's why I'm asking. Is Roberta in the bathroom?"

"No, sir. I haven't seen stupid Roberta. Probably in the wrong room."

"Now, Betty, remember, we don't call each other names."

Betty hung her head and went to her room without another word. Mr. B went to Roberta's room and knocked. When Roberta didn't answer he tried again. Then he cracked the door open and called softly. He stuck his head in. Empty. He went back out into the hall and called her name. The others in the kitchen stopped what they were doing and looked around.

He called louder. Betty and Julie stuck their heads out of their respective rooms.

"Has anybody seen Roberta?" he asked.

Now Mr. B began to worry. He had seen her when she had fallen out of bed, but not since. He hurriedly searched the house, all the time calling her name. She was missing. Forgetting about the broken office door, Mr. B called Mrs. Anderson.

***

Justin's mother stood across the street from the school looking up and down the road in front. Nobody would be there this time of the morning. Where would he hide? The playground? She crossed the street and continued behind the school sweeping the area with her eyes. She could see the soccer fields and small track inside the chain link fencing. Just past the far end, she thought she could see bright colors that would indicate some type of playground equipment. She walked over to the fenced in area where the swings and merry-go-round sat. The gate was closed and locked. She checked a set of doors to the school and found them securely locked. She didn't want to knock and arouse any kind of watchman.

Had he walked the streets all night? If someone had picked him up, they would have called. She turned and walked away from the silent playground, back past the rear of the school. When she heard a motor start, she instinctively turned toward the sound. A big sheet metal box with ductwork running every which way rumbled. As she turned away, a flash of white caught her eye. She stopped, turned back, and walked toward the out of place swatch. There, tucked tightly between the two big boxes, slept Justin. She could feel the uncontrollable anger well up inside. How dare he run away from her! How dare he try to duck his punishment! She let the wooden handle slip out of her sleeve. Her fingers found their usual grip on the well-worn, shortened broomstick.

***

Roberta happily chatted away at all the sights she saw from the bus windows. Davy looked, but his mind was elsewhere. He just wanted to get it done. Find Justin and head for the mountains. They could be at Protection in less than three go-arounds on his watch. Before the bus came to a halt at the stop, Davy strained to see Justin. As soon as it stopped, he jumped up and hurried off the bus. Roberta watched for a second then jumped up and ran up the aisle to catch up. As soon as his feet hit the ground he looked around. His heart fell when he didn't see Justin. Davy moved to the corner and looked up the street that Justin had come from the last time he saw him. A single car passed by the other way. Maybe he's just out of sight, Davy thought. Then he looked at his watch. The big hand had past the top. Not by much, but maybe too much for Justin or maybe he had overslept. Roberta caught up with him.

"What are we here for?" she asked.

"Justin was supposed to meet me here," Davy replied.

"Where is he?" she asked.

"I don't know," he replied looking back up and down all the streets for the third time.

"I don't see anyone," she said looking around, too.

"He might be late," Davy said without taking his eyes off the street.

Roberta went over to the bench at the bus stop and sat down.

"Well. If he's not here, then what?"

Davy paced back and forth looking up and down the street, listening to the constant questions from Roberta.

"Just be quiet, Roberta," he said louder than he wanted.

"Don't yell at me Davy," she shot back.

Davy saw her face getting red as it did whenever she started getting mad.

He didn't know what to do. His mind began getting all fluttery as he tried to think. Then Davy felt something. It touched him so softly he wasn't sure it was anything. He stood mulling the feeling over in his head. He thought that maybe the feeling came from Justin. He turned in a circle trying to pinpoint the source.

"What are you doing now?" Roberta said.

"Shush just a moment," Davy hissed at her.

"Don't you tell me—" Roberta started. She stopped when Davy glared at her.

Davy closed his eyes again. He turned until he thought he faced the source. When he opened his eyes he was looking straight across the street at the school. It must be coming from behind it, he thought. Then he felt a spike, pain and fear in the feeling. Davy started walking quickly, almost at a jog, hoping to find the source of the feeling before it disappeared. Roberta, who sat on the bench with her arms folded and a scowl on her face, watched him for a moment. When he walked across the street, she got off the bench and stomped after him. Davy crossed the large green lawn in front of the school and started moving along side of the brick building. When he reached the corner on the front side of the school, he stopped to check the feeling again. Roberta caught up with him and stopped beside him, panting. Before she even had a chance to ask, he took off even faster down along side of the school. She wanted to tell him to slow down, but she couldn't catch her breath enough to even speak. She walked as fast as she could, trying to catch up. He rounded the corner behind the school. She started getting scared that he may forget all about her and continued right out of sight. She'd be lost. A wave of relief swept through her when she saw him stop on the corner. Then just as she got close enough to yell, she saw him stiffen just before he went out of sight.

Davy heard someone yelling Justin's name, not in a good way. He felt that familiar pressure on his bladder as he became frightened. It came from behind the school.

***

Mrs. Anderson told Mr. B she would come right away. She wasted little time in calling the police from her house. Better to find Roberta later wandering in the back yard or on the block somewhere than to give her a bigger head start in the city by not calling them. She was a girl after all. A bit heavy, but perverts preyed on anyone and Roberta would make an easy target. The police responded quickly, putting out a call for a young heavy-set girl answering to Roberta. Mrs. Anderson jumped in her car and drove to the home while Mr. B continued the search inside. He couldn't leave the others to check outside, although he did look out all the windows and called out from the front and back porch. All the other residents started to act out. Betty skipped around the house singing. "Bye bye, Roberta birdy. Bye bye to you." The others joined in, laughing the whole time.

***

Justin was dreaming. He found himself rolled up in a blanket so tight he couldn't move and in a place he didn't recognize. He wasn't scared because the blanket felt warm and comfortable. He wanted to go back to his dream sleep, but he couldn't. Something made too much noise. A loud explosion woke him, followed by that terrible sound of his name coming from the mouth of his angry drunken mother. His initial reaction was to squeeze into a tighter ball. He felt his heart banging in his throat. Finally the dream vanished and he remembered. He looked up to try and locate her. He tried to focus but his vision wouldn't clear. He saw a blurry shape of several colors moving in front of him. Then he felt the wind from her stick just missing the top of his head and crashing into the ductwork with a resounding bang. His mother's screaming voice quickly replaced the ringing in his ears.

"Justin! Get out of there! Justin! Come here right now!"

All Justin could do was squeeze back further into the gap his mother couldn't fit into. He knew that sooner or later she would find a way to reach him and he knew he wouldn't be able to run any more. He buried his head on his knees and began to cry. He jumped as another loud bang rattled his head. Suddenly things got quiet. His mother no longer yelled and the club stopped bouncing off the hollow tin. He heard the small stones crunching under her feet as she moved to the side looking for a way to reach him. He couldn't look up to find her, he didn't dare. He knew she had found a way to get closer and his head remained exposed from above. He covered it with his thin arms and tried to make himself even smaller. Then he couldn't hear her moving anymore. He listened carefully for her footsteps. The silence frightened him. Finally he peeked up from his protective ball, keeping his head covered with his hands. She wasn't anywhere around and he began to uncurl to try and peer over the duct.

When the first blow broke his wrist, he fainted. The last thing he remembered was hearing the triumph in his mother's voice coming from above him. She had climbed up on the housing and managed to get over top of him.

"There you little bastard. Try and hide from me!"

Justin's mother had gone black with rage. Spittle flew from her mouth and her hair flew wildly. Justin had turned into a small version of her ex-husband, now trapped and defenseless. She was going to give back all she had ever taken, both physically and mentally. She raised her club again already marking the spot she would hit when a voice stopped her.

"Hey lady! You stop that! Stop right now!"

She turned and saw some fat retard waddling toward her. His face looked beet red and his mouth hung open and panting. She couldn't believe that someone would interfere just when her revenge was almost complete. She crawled back down from the duct and turned toward the oncoming dummy. Well, if he wanted a piece of what she was handing out then so be it. As soon as he got close enough, she would level him and then she could get back to her ex and finish that job.

***

Roberta stood at the same corner Davy had disappeared around with her hands on her knees. Her lungs burned and her legs wobbled. She thought she might pass out. She saw a bench and collapsed on it, this time leaning back and sucking in all the air she could. She started getting angry with Davy for leaving her behind. She wanted to go after him but she needed to slow her breathing a bit. She thought she might be having a heart attack. When her breathing slowed, she noticed the yelling coming from behind the building. It sounded angry. Roberta forced herself to her feet and started in the direction Davy had gone.

***

Davy saw the woman come down off the big silver box. She walked a few steps in his direction and then stopped, facing him. He slowed his pace. He had lost touch with Justin when he saw the last blow land. He didn't know what it meant. He had yelled at the woman. He never did that before. In fact he had never yelled at another adult in his life. But he never had trust before, he thought. He didn't see any adults around to help him stop this woman from beating Justin with a club. It made him angry. Davy walked right past her without making eye contact to check on Justin. Like Roberta, he tried to catch his breath from running. Suddenly everything went black with the exception of several bright pinpricks of light. His knees buckled and he felt himself going down. He instinctively reached for the ground to cushion his fall. He got scared when he realized that the woman had hit him even though he felt little pain. Davy had been hit before when he had been going to the regular school. Then he had curled into a ball to protect himself and it had worked so he repeated the action now. The next blow hit him in the back. The sting raced through him. His body wanted to straighten out as a reflex to the attack. Davy just kicked out with his feet and covered his head even more as he waited for the next blow. Instead he heard a grunt and a heavy tinny bang. He stayed in his fetal position, unwilling to expose his head.

***

Roberta supported herself by leaning against the school wall while her mind tried to absorb what she saw. She noticed Davy right away, still leaving her behind but moving slower. She also saw a woman standing there looking at Davy, looking mean. Her hair stuck out all over like she had been caught in a wind. Her clothes looked bunched and dirty. The look on her face scared Roberta. She had a wide eyed and crazed look Roberta associated with some of the people she had seen when she went to group homes where people sometimes screamed at no one and pulled their hair out in clumps. Then she saw the woman's eyes close into slits. Roberta started to call to Davy when she saw the woman turn with her club raised. Everything went into slow motion. Roberta knew what came next and she wanted to yell, to tell him to watch out. Nothing came as Roberta froze, even her labored breathing had stopped. She saw the stick come down hard and she could hear the cold thump of wood on flesh, the same sound she heard in the kitchen when they tenderized steaks. It landed on the back of Davy's neck and she watched him crumble. Roberta stretched out her hand as if to grab him and hold him up, but she was a good thirty yards away. She staggered toward him like she had been hit herself. She still didn't understand what she saw. Again the club went up and Roberta froze once more. Why was the woman attacking Davy with the club? She watched it come down in an arc and connect with Davy's back. She saw his feet fly out in reaction to the blow. The same sickening sound of wood on meat reached her ears. Worse yet, the woman wasn't finished. Roberta saw the club being raised again. Now it was Roberta's eyes that narrowed.

SIXTEEN

The ulasiga recoiled in the bowels of his lair. Something wasn't right. It had been feeling a faint input from the man since he had left the cave. Although the man stayed too far for direct communication, there still remained a sympathetic link. Now it felt nothing. Of course the ulasiga had no complex emotions to attach to this; no sorrow, no worry. The ulasiga only knew pain and the sudden loss of communication caused a reflex. Soon it relaxed. It had to save its energy for the next trip to the surface.

***

Roberta got angry, real angry. First she got mad at herself for not stopping the first blow. Then she got angry with the woman for hitting Davy. When the woman lifted her club to hit Davy again, she saw herself pushing the woman, hard. The woman flew backwards into the big metal boxes, where she hit hard and collapsed on the ground. The sound of her hitting the tin echoed off the school wall. Roberta stood there for a moment glaring at the crumpled form of the woman, waiting for her to move. When she didn't, Roberta hurried over to Davy. Her lungs didn't seem to work very well and a wheezing sound escaped whenever she inhaled. Davy wasn't moving and she began to get scared.

"Davy!" she panted.

She had to take several more breaths before she could continue and then she had to take a breath in between each word.

"Davy-uh-uh-you-uh-uh-okay-uh-uh-Davy?"

Her heart hammered in her chest and she started getting dizzy. Over her shoulder she could heard a small voice calling Davy.

"Davy? Davy?"

Davy heard both voices and finally uncovered his head. He looked past Roberta searching out the crazy woman that had hit him. He saw her lying by the big silver boxes. He got to his feet slowly.

Roberta looked at Davy and then the little boy. With so much going on, Roberta couldn't focus on either. She stayed bent over gasping for air.

Davy saw Justin coming toward him. He noticed the boy walked funny, kind of like the bums on the street. Justin wasn't moving very steady and he had a big lump on his forehead, a little trail of blood running from it. He held his arm, the wrist limp and dangling. He could also feel the anguish pouring from the small boy, fresh hurt.

Davy stepped back first and then moved quickly past Roberta toward Justin. The aura of fear had staggered him as much as the blow to the back of his neck. He turned pale as the blood drained from his face. He felt the hurt but it was fractured, coming from all over the boy. He couldn't feel Justin's bruises and the broken wrist but he could feel the pain in the form of waves coming from different parts of his body. Those black clouds of hurt from physical pain paled in comparison to the sickness in the boy's heart. A dark cold spot of hopelessness sat inside Justin. Davy wanted to remove it, fix it, do something to help. He had never felt such a mixture of fright, pain, and loss coming from a child. One bright spot flared. Davy felt a pinprick of hope inside the boy. Tears filled Davy's eyes and ran down his cheeks. He sent as much comfort as he could into the boy. He looked for his eyes and noticed they, too, weren't quite right and then they closed. Justin collapsed on the pavement.

Roberta shot past Davy and snatched Justin up in her arms. Even she was surprised at how quickly she moved when just a few seconds ago she felt on the verge of collapse. Roberta turned toward Davy with Justin limp as a doll in her arms.

"Who is this? Davy! Make him feel better!"

"It's Justin, the boy I'm taking to Protection. I can't Roberta. He has to look at me."

"Try anyway Davy. Try something. He's so little. He's so hurt."

Davy looked at the poor boy, lying there in Roberta's arms. Davy got frightened that maybe Justin was dead. He focused his mind inside and sent a wave of warmth and comfort. Immediately he saw Justin's eyes flutter. He could feel a small change from within the boy. I can do it without seeing their eyes, he thought.

Justin's mother groaned and both Davy and Roberta turned. Roberta prepared to push her again when she heard Davy.

"We got to go right now. Come on Roberta! Now!"

Roberta turned back and followed Davy with Justin still in her arms. Davy zigzagged up and down streets and across alleys as quick as he could. He made sure to avoid the main streets where he thought the police might patrol. After a few blocks, he took Justin from a grateful Roberta and continued his non-stop weaving and twisting. Roberta began to think that Davy had got them all lost. She looked at the houses and they all looked the same. We're right back where we started, she thought. She half expected to see the school and that awful woman.

She caught up with Davy and peeked over his shoulder. She could see Justin starting to stir. Davy made a sharp turn into a park and found a bench deep inside behind a big tree. He gently set Justin down on it. Roberta sat beside him and pulled him to her side. Davy got down on his knees and peered up into his face.

"Justin? Justin? Can you hear me?"

Justin tried to lift his head and for just a moment smiled.

Davy reached into his pack and took out a bottle of water and held it out for Justin. Roberta took it from him and pulled Justin over like she saw mothers do on television. She put the bottle slowly to his lips and dribbled a few drops out. Justin pulled up his head and sucked on the bottle taking a couple small sips of the water. Roberta pulled it away to make sure he didn't choke. Justin kept his eyes closed but smiled.

"Are you hungry?" asked Davy.

He saw a small nod, eyes still closed.

Davy searched his pack and found a small snack bag of jelly fruits. He took one out. It was cherry, Davy's favorite. He put it to Justin's lips and watched as Justin nibbled on it.

"This is one of the children you're saving. This is Justin," said Roberta.

Davy looked up in surprise.

"You remember?"

"Sure!"

Then Roberta thought about it. She started finding things in her mind she didn't know existed. She looked at Davy, who stared at her.

"Spaghetti, you dumb old stockboy."

Davy started laughing and Roberta joined in.

"You can remember things, Roberta!"

Roberta just grinned from ear to ear. They both looked at Justin and saw he had his eyes open. He smiled, too, although it was a crooked smile, like one side of his face wasn't working quite right.

***

"Hey, Marshall, whadda ya say we ride behind the school and check the playground for the retard?" said Ben, one of the city cops.

"Don't you mean the mentally challenged?" asked his partner.

"Yeah, like you. Mentally challenged."

Marshall laughed. "Have to be, to work with a dead weight like you. The girl lived thirty blocks from here. She wouldn't be all the way over here."

"Let's check it out anyway."

The policemen pulled their cruiser into the rear parking lot of the school. The playground looked empty.

"Hey, Ben! There! On your right."

Ben looked over and saw a woman standing by the big ventilation units. She tried to hold herself steady against the big metal boxes. He could see her clothing rumpled and twisted out of place and her hair looked like it had been exposed to high voltage.

Ben turned the car and drove over to her. Marshall called in to report. They both got out and cautiously walked over to her. She stood there leaning up against the big duct unit for support. They could see her trying to hold herself steady. She looked around like she was missing something. The police split apart and moved up on either side. Ben reached out and carefully removed the broomstick from her hand and set it up on the metal ductwork. They both grabbed an arm.

"Are you alright, Miss?"

"He's gone. They took him."

"Took who, Miss?"

"My son. They took my son."

Ben looked over at Marshall and caught his eye. He then shot a look down at the front of the woman. Marshall followed the gaze and saw blood spots on her shirt. He looked back at Ben who then cocked his head toward the broom handle. Marshall understood. They both led the unsteady woman to the car and placed her in the back seat. Once away from the woman, Ben spoke first.

"Dude, there's blood and a few hairs on that club she was holding."

"On her shirt, too," said Marshall.

"She's drunker than a Mick on St. Patty's day."

"What about her boy that she keeps mumbling about?"

"We better call this in. By the looks of things, he's probably at home, dead."

SEVENTEEN

Davy fed Justin a few more bits of the gummy fruit candies and gave him some sips of water in between.

"When does your pass say you have to be back?" Davy asked Roberta.

When she didn't say anything, Davy looked over and immediately recognized the blank stare. Davy sighed. Here he had thought a miracle had happened, but maybe it had just been a lucky moment. Suddenly Roberta's eyes lit up and she reached into her pocket. She pulled out not one but two bright yellow passes. Davy took them from her and looked at them. No date, no time, no signature. He looked back up at Roberta.

"These aren't signed."

"I know. Mrs. Anderson wouldn't give me one."

"How'd you get out of the house?"

"I was on my way to ask Mr. B about them. He was acting strange. He just stood in front of the office door, opening and closing it. He was funny."

"Roberta! How did you get out without a pass?"

"Oh, yeah. I was walking down the hall and I saw you standing outside so I just went out the door. I only came out to say hi and have you come in, but you just said 'come on' and started leaving."

"Why didn't you tell me you didn't have a pass? They'll call, you know. The police will be looking for you."

"Why? I didn't do anything wrong."

"Not to arrest you, silly. Mrs. Anderson won't want you out wandering around all alone."

"Oh! What should I do? Go back?"

"You should. I have to take Justin and we have to stay hidden, away from the big roads. We can't get caught by the police. They will take Justin away and maybe me, too, for having him. I have to get him to Protection."

"Well, let's go then. Where is it?"

"You can't go Roberta. It's too far and you'll be in big trouble. Plus if we see the police, we'll have to run. They'll be looking for you."

"I'm supposed to help you. You promised. Besides, I'm not leaving. This little boy won't be able to keep up. I can help you carry him."

"It's far away and now we can't take the bus. We'll have to walk. Can you make it a long ways?"

"I can go as far as you, Davy!"

"Well, it's in the mountains, up the Black Trail," he said, his voice dropping. He pulled his card out of his pocket and showed her the black spot. Davy expected to see Roberta recoil from the card much the same as he did. She simply ignored it and pushed it away, uninterested.

"Which way is it?"

Davy turned and looked over the distant landscape, slowly, trying to decide. Suddenly he stopped and pointed.

"Up there," he said.

Roberta looked where he pointed away from the city and to the hazy mountains. It didn't seem very far.

Roberta looked down at the little face beside her. Taking a napkin from Davy's hand and a little water from the bottle, she gently wiped it clean.

"Can you walk?" she asked Justin.

He nodded his head and tried to stand while holding his hurt wrist against his chest for support. He stumbled a bit and wavered, reminding Roberta of the brand new baby horses she saw on TV. Davy reached out a hand to steady the boy before he fell. Davy fashioned a crude sling for Justin's arm from an extra windbreaker he kept in his pack.

"How 'bout I give you a piggyback ride?" he asked Justin.

Justin looked up at him with that weird half smile and nodded his head. Davy bent over and Roberta helped Justin up on his back. Davy turned and started off in the direction of the mountain. Roberta grabbed the backpack and followed.

"Is it okay, Davy?" asked Roberta. "He's not too heavy is he?"

"He doesn't weigh much more than the back pack and I've been hiking all summer. You just stay close behind and if you see any police cars you tell me. If you can't keep up, just say so."

Roberta looked around quickly at the mention of police cars. "I don't see any!"

They walked twenty blocks through the mostly residential streets. Davy led them down alleys and ran quickly across the major thoroughfares leaving the shops and small stores behind as they moved into the foothills. They turned off the sidewalks and went behind buildings to avoid cars that they thought might be police. As the city woke up, they encountered more and more people. They got several curious looks from people washing cars and mowing lawns. They made a strange trio. Still, they continued their trek.

***

The ulasiga pulled itself into a single mass in its lair. It could feel the man Davy again and knew he moved toward the cave. The creature didn't know the reason for the previous loss of connection, it only knew it had returned. At the Davy's current pace, the ulasiga had plenty of time before he arrived. The ulasiga sucked up some nourishment from its stores and then began the journey through the cracks and crevices of the rock, moving slowly toward the surface, back to the cave where the prey should deliver the meal. The ulasiga replayed the scene it had built the last time. It would have to project it again. It became anxious to download more memories and new ones from the new man it would bring. It moved tentatively on its journey, feeling for any unanticipated light. It remembered the sudden searing pain of the last encounter and how quickly the light had struck and then disappeared. The ulasiga had no knowledge of such a light. It still didn't understand how it came and went so fast. Maybe man could be more dangerous than it had thought. The ulasiga would search the memory for light and perhaps learn the secret.

The lure of a large meal overrode the fear of the sudden encounter with light. Cell, leap frogging over cell, the ulasiga stretched its way through the cold blackness.

***

Davy had to stop. The road had been climbing steadily as he left the city behind. He found a spot off the road by a stream rushing down from the mountain. He wanted to step in it and cool his tired feet, but he had gotten his feet wet before and remembered the blisters he got hiking with wet socks. He gently set Justin down on his back in a patch of high, brown grass. The sunny day had warmed considerably. He looked at the boy who appeared even smaller than before. He looked pale and barely conscious. Roberta dropped down beside Justin, sweat beading on her forehead and her shirt. Davy handed her the water and she took a long drink. He reached up and stopped her arm.

"That's all I have, Roberta. We have to save it for the trip back."

"But there's a bunch of water right there in the river."

"You can't drink that water."

"Why not?"

"Cause animals poop in it."

Roberta started to giggle. Davy turned beet red and then started to get mad.

"What's so funny?"

"You said 'poop.'"

Roberta laughed harder.

"Now I said it," she repeated.

Davy relaxed and joined in with the joke.

They both turned to Justin and Roberta handed him the water.

"Davy, tell me about where we're going," Roberta asked.

Davy looked at her for a moment. How could he tell her? Would she believe? Understand? Did it matter?

He reached into his pack and brought out the little lunch snacks. He opened them and gave two to Roberta. He kept one and made a little sandwich out of the cracker and cheese. Roberta broke the little crackers into small pieces and gave them to Justin to eat. She placed tiny bits into his mouth and she made sure he drank plenty to keep him from choking. Davy began his story about the trip he had made to Protection only a week ago. Roberta listened, spell bound, as she let her imagination build. He told her of the crying child only to find a bird made the sound and then being scared that he would get lost. He told her of the storm that drove him inside the cave and the feeling that there was someone else inside. He told her of Mr. Harrington and the promise he had made.

"It's responsibility, Roberta. I have to help and I have to do it."

Roberta swelled with happiness. Her Davy was important. She hadn't known anyone that important. Of course Mrs. Anderson and Mr. B were important but not in the same way. This was the first special person she ever knew trusted to do something so dangerous.

"You, too, Roberta. You have a responsibility, too."

Roberta's mouth dropped open as she realized what Davy said. She was here, too. She was helping Davy take poor Justin to Protection, that wonderful place in the mountains. That made her important. She looked back at Davy with wide eyes.

"Shut your mouth Roberta or I'll think I've found the cave."

She slammed it shut and for a second her anger and embarrassment flared until she saw the smile on Davy's face.

"You're a butthead, Davy"

"It's time to go. We still have a ways to travel and it won't stay light forever."

"You want me to carry him for a while?" asked Roberta.

Davy looked up at the hill to the top of the peaks. Somehow he knew just how far he had to go.

"Okay. You carry him along the road and then when we get to the parking lot, I'll take him."

***

Phil Maloney had been a cop for six years. He joined because he needed a job and he qualified. Simple. He never had a burning desire to join Law Enforcement and he never really developed that 'BoohYa!' some of the others got. Nine to five, some weekends, get over yourself, can't save the world fit on his partial list of do's and don'ts. Don't get stupid, gung-ho, or dead also made it. He had a wife and two little ones at home.

Three more hours till shift change. It had been a quiet easy morning and it was still early enough on Saturday that the road wouldn't have any drunks and few speeders. Lunch time had arrived and he drove down through the pass on his way to Bleacher's where he could get a couple of salsa dogs, fries, and a coke. He called it his fifteen mile-an-hour lunch.

Anyone driving less than fifteen miles-an-hour over the speed limit had a free pass. Phil knew that anyone he stopped now would eat away some of his lunch hour. He knew he could spend his day with speeders, but he used them to fill the gaps of boredom while looking for the more serious violators. Drunks, druggies, and criminals usually stayed within the speed limit. If he wanted to catch the dangerous ones, he would have to stay on the highway watching, not writing out a ticket to some poor schmuck going five miles over.

Besides, ten over was the norm and his stomach growled. 'Don't miss lunch' suddenly made it to his list of do's and don'ts.

Phil crested a small rise in his marked cruiser just before the last down slope into the city. He drove about sixty-five on the winding mountain road, a bit fast perhaps, but he owned the road and he did enjoy the feel of the heavy car swooping into the curves. His eyes landed on two people walking up the road on the opposite side; a couple of hippos, waddling up the hill. Well, that'll take a few pounds off them, he thought, although he rarely saw people on foot climbing up along the east bound side. As he went by he looked across the road. He checked the guy, first noticing the yellow shirt and black pants, huffing and puffing. Then, a sweeping look at the girl behind him, red jacket and brown pants. God-awful combo there. It was only a quick glance because the people in front of him had a tendency to hit their brakes when they noticed him coming up behind. Rear-ending a civilian would definitely ruin his lunch. Then another glance as he went past. At first he thought the girl wore some kind of strange backpack. Phil did a double take and saw a kid instead, riding the girl piggyback style. Ouch! That had to add to the climb. The girls face was a mask of red as she strained to make the grade.

Phil became a cop because he needed a job but that didn't mean he wasn't good at it. Over the years he had learned the same lessons as the cops before him. Dealing with the public builds up a sixth sense of right and wrong. Something didn't appear quite right; the way the girl reached out and tugged on the man's sleeve; the way she tracked Phil's passing with her eyes; and then the eyes themselves struck him as strange. All of this registered in a microsecond as Phil continued to speed down the hill. He instinctively hit his brakes and checked his rearview mirror to see the reaction. People avoiding the police will bolt when the brakes come on. He didn't see any change although the girl still watched. Phil turned his attention back to the road as his mind peeked under the corners of the problem to see if the answer lay there. A growl from his stomach erased the issue. Two tubbys and their kid, how dangerous could they be? Phil shook his head. Never miss lunch he repeated.

EIGHTEEN

"It's a policeman," Roberta whispered.

Davy thought he heard Roberta say something but his own panting jumbled her words. He continued to trudge up the hill. Then he felt Roberta tugging on his sleeve. He almost stopped walking but he knew the trailhead parking lot sat right around the corner. He could sit down, catch his breath and deal with Roberta all at the same time.

"They're stopping."

Davy heard, "When are we stopping?"

He continued his pace without pause. Only a hundred more yards to the parking lot, he thought.

Roberta watched the police car continue down the highway. She turned back toward Davy and saw that he had already moved several steps ahead. She hurried to catch up, her own labored breathing getting worse as she felt Justin bobbing up and down on her back. She glanced back once more and the car had gone. Roberta turned back and continued to follow Davy up the hill. Her earlier excitement at being part of his important job faded as her legs weakened and the sweat rolled into her eyes. She plodded step by step, the police forgotten. Now she just looked down at the road and watched her feet move one in front of the other. She used the image of a pale and sick Justin to keep moving.

"Roberta! Over here."

She stopped and looked up. Davy had disappeared. She turned toward his voice and saw him sitting on the bench at the bus stop. She looked at the big parking area and saw half a dozen cars parked about. She hurried over and Davy took Justin from her, setting him on the bench. He laid there, eyes closed and breathing lightly.

"Davy, he doesn't look too good. He's awful pale. And feel his forehead; it's cold and wet. He isn't even hiking. He shouldn't be wet."

"Yeah, he doesn't look very good," he said as his eyes turned toward the mountains.

"Try to wake him up."

Davy reached out and shook him lightly, then patted his cheek while calling his name. Justin's eyes fluttered for a moment and then he smiled his crooked smile.

"Uh we aah Patecshun?" he slurred.

"Not yet Justin, but it won't be long. Just an hour or so. You hang on. You want some water?"

Justin closed his eyes and nodded his head. Davy tipped the bottle to his mouth and watched as Justin took a few swallows. Roberta pulled her shirt tail from her pants and poured some water on it, then used it to wipe Justin's face. Davy looked up at her and saw the love and tenderness on her face as she ministered to Justin. She will make a good mom, he thought. He could feel his heart swell and the new feeling scared him for a moment.

"We have to get going Roberta. There's a water fountain over there near where the trail starts. Can you fill the bottle back up?"

"Did you see the policeman, Davy? I thought he was going to stop."

Davy turned his head quickly toward the entrance expecting to see flashing lights and men with guns drawn. Roberta saw him jump at what she said. She reached out and grabbed his shoulder to hold him from getting up.

"No, Davy. When we were walking up here. He went the other way." Roberta thought that would settle Davy, but it didn't. Davy grabbed Justin and started walking quickly toward the trail. Roberta, again, had to almost run to keep up. Davy went up the trail a few feet until the lot and highway disappeared behind the trees.

"What's the matter?" Roberta asked.

"We can't have the police stop us," Davy said. "They would take Justin back to his mother, take you back to the home, and take me to jail."

"No they wouldn't. You're doing a good thing aren't you?"

"They wouldn't understand."

"Well, I won't let them."

Davy looked up and smiled. Roberta had certainly changed since he picked her up this morning. Today had been more excitement than they had in their entire lives. He held out the water bottle again.

"Stay with Justin till I fill this up and come back."

Roberta sat down and held Justin in her lap. She brushed his hair from his forehead being careful not to touch the bump on his head. She noticed it going down a bit, still Justin didn't seem well. She hoped the place had doctors. She looked down at his face and studied it carefully. Once she saw past the bruises and dark circles under his eyes, she could see the angel inside of him. She saw how beautiful and perfect he looked. She felt she could sit there forever and just look at him. A tear fell from her eye and splashed on his face. She saw him try to smile and lift his arm as if to brush it away, but it fell back to his side. Roberta reached out with her finger and dried the wet spot for him. Davy came back and stood there for just a second and watched them. Again he felt funny in his heart. Maybe it's a heart attack, he thought. Well, if it feels this good, why would people be so afraid of them, he wondered.

"Come on, Roberta. Time to go."

Davy's eyes went wide when she looked up and he saw she was crying.

"Roberta, what's the matter? Why're you crying?"

"Davy, he's so pretty. I feel so bad for him. Is there a doctor at this place?"

"I'm sure there is," he said trying not to ask himself the same question. Mr. Harrington wasn't a doctor and the two other children weren't either. It didn't matter. Mr. Harrington would know what to do.

Roberta slowly stood up feeling her legs protest.

"How much longer do we have to walk? Is it close?"

"I'm not real sure. Maybe an hour."

Roberta helped put Justin up on Davy's back and the three started up the trail again.

***

The ulasiga could feel the man Davy coming closer. It wouldn't be long now. It had never been sure of a meal before. Now with the absolute certainty of food, the ulasiga traveled closer to the cave. It stopped just short of the crack that opened into the chamber where the man would bring its meal and where it could replay the memories. The ulasiga pushed out some signals to the carrier hoping to help guide him back and to prepare him for re-entry into the fantasy the ulasiga had built.

***

Phil sat at the counter inside Bleacher's with two steaming salsa dogs in front of him. He could smell the Jalapenos and just a hint of lime. Before he could grip the first one, two city cops came in and sat beside him. They looked somewhat familiar. He had probably seen them in here before. He nodded to them and they returned the same without a smile. Phil grabbed the first dog and took a big bite, filling his mouth full. He slowly chewed, mixing in the salsa with the beef and bread, trying to separate all the individual flavors and mixing them together at the same time. This is why you never miss lunch, he told himself. The two cops beside him were engaged in shoptalk and Phil couldn't help but overhear the conversation. A good cop listens.

"You think she killed him?"

"Sure. You saw the blood and the stick."

"How come they didn't find a body?"

"She probably dumped it in some pond. It'll show up in a few weeks just like this girl here."

The cop next to Phil tossed a photo up on the counter. Phil scanned it from the corner of his eye as he took another large chunk out of his dog.

"You think she's dead?"

"A girl? A retard? In this town? If not yet, then soon, unless she wanders into the right place."

Phil went back to his meal. Those eyes looked familiar, he thought to himself. But the girl he saw hadn't been alone. Couldn't be her. He looked at his second hot dog as his mind battled between the photo on the counter, which might be the girl hiking up the road, and the food in front of him.

Never miss lunch became secondary to duty, besides, the first dog settled into the empty pit reducing the urgency. He turned to the cops next to him.

"Who's this?" he asked tapping the photo.

Both cops turned and looked at him. He could see the invisible wall start to go up. Even though they were all in law enforcement, they still protected their territory. City, state, federal, they all remained loyal to their own first. When the two city cops saw what he pointed to, they relaxed. Phil knew they didn't care who found runaways. Once they did though, then jurisdiction would be established.

"A girl reported missing this morning," said Marshall.

Ben leaned around him and added, "Yeah, some retard escaped from the group home. Probably wandering in the back yard lost as Robinson Caruso."

"Where's the home at?"

"Canyon Rim area. Ya seen her?"

"I saw someone like her, but she had some guy with her and a kid. They were walking up the Bates Canyon Road. Any description on her clothing?"

"Not that we got. The report said she had missed head count in the morning, but had been seen minutes before. It's a home for Down syndrome and other kids with learning disabilities, not real serious cases."

"She a runaway or they think she was taken?"

"They don't know for sure. With these kids it's always hard to tell. They're easy pickings for the perverts."

"Thanks. I think I'll check out the one I saw just in case."

"Good luck. Want me to finish that other dog for ya?" asked Ben.

"If you can pry it from my cold dead fingers," replied Phil with a smile as he wrapped it in a napkin.

Phil tossed a five on the counter and left. Inside his cruiser, he brought up his computer and found the info on the missing girl while he finished the second dog. Roberta Roberts, eighteen, resides at a home for children in the 3000 block of Canyon Rim, missing since eight thirty this morning. Five foot three, one hundred fifty pounds. The picture scrolled up. It was the same as the boys in the restaurant had shown him. He could see the round face and eyes. Unmistakable. He tried to imagine five foot three and one hundred fifty pounds. Did the size fit? He wasn't sure. He had been focused on the eyes that had tracked him as he went by. Well, they couldn't have gone very far hiking up that road, he thought. He put his car in gear and went back the way he came.

NINETEEN

Roberta looked up the wide and well-worn Black Trail that wound its way through the tall trees, some already devoid of leaves as fall passed quickly. The tall pines reminded Roberta of Christmas. Roberta looked at the large tree trunks along the trail and saw a black paint splotch on a nearby aspen. Excitedly, she yanked Davy's sleeve.

"There's a black dot, Davy."

"I see it. We have to follow them for awhile, but then we have to go that way," he said pointing up and to the right.

It didn't take long before Roberta could feel her legs getting tired again. She tried to muster up that strength using the earlier excitement of knowing both Davy and her had been given an important mission. It helped a little.

Davy also strained up the path. Even though Justin weighed the same as his backpack he carried on the hikes he had taken in the summer, the lack of sleep, the running fear, and worry of the last twenty-four hours wore on him. He knew exactly where he had to go and somehow he also knew he shouldn't know. He remembered being confused and scared when he had left the trail and that he had been lost just before he found the cave. There had been no splotches of any color. Was his mind playing tricks? Would he get them lost instead of to Protection? He opened his mind to try to feel the children there. He felt the tiny signal, just enough to follow.

He worried a lot about Justin. He could feel the boy rolling in and out of consciousness as they went up the trail. He could feel the black pain and then strangely enough, joy would flow through his thoughts. It felt like the little glittering waves on the pond in the park.

Justin dreamed of Protection. At first he saw a door open up to a place full of light. He could see children playing and toys everywhere. It felt warm and soft inside and everyone smiled at him. He moved through the huge rooms. Carnival rides along a brightly lit midway appeared and he heard the music of a merry-go-round. Then he saw his mother and froze for just a moment. He noticed that she wasn't drunk, but happy and smiling. She stood there with her arms outstretched, reaching for him. She looked better, sober, happy! Davy stood there, too, with his big smiling eyes and funny grin. Davy waved to him to hurry in. Justin tried to run to them but his legs wouldn't move. They felt stiff and he didn't have the strength to lift them. Then the door to Protection started to close. He yelled for help and reached out his hands, but his mother and Davy just continued to stand there smiling and waving. He quickly tried to grasp the handle on the door, but he was too slow and too late. The door slammed shut and the lights all went out. Darkness enveloped him. From behind, he felt something cold, something hungry, and it came for him. He turned to find the source of the terror, but he couldn't see it in the blackness. Still, he could hear it moving across the rocks, a long drawn out hiss, like wet scales along gravel. It moved slowly and began to circle him, whispering his name. A chill shot through him as he felt something touch his sneaker. It crept slowly up his shoe. He wanted to kick, to fling it off but his legs had turned to dead weights. Then its cold wet arm wrapped around his ankle and began to pull him deeper toward the darkness. Justin reached out and gripped the handle to the door of Protection. He held on with all of his might, straining as his fingers began to slip. He felt the breath of the monster, cold and wet as fog; the odor foul and gut wrenching.

The door slowly began to open as Justin felt his arms about to pull away. A small spill of light escaped the crack, carrying the joyful sounds and smells of Protection. Justin looked down toward his foot to see what had him. It looked like clear jelly, slimy and cold, like the stuff kids brought to school to play with. It had wrapped around his shoe and pulled him. Then a face began to form. It had an open gaping mouth full of razor sharp teeth. Eyes began to break through the liquid like mass. As the image coalesced, Justin saw the face of his raging mother.

***

Roberta looked up and saw Justin's leg jerking and his head turning back and forth. She hurried up to Davy and again she found his sleeve.

"Davy! Justin is having a bad dream."

Davy could feel the fear sweeping through the boy. He paused to look at Roberta, then turned back toward the direction of the cave feeling the urge to continue. Something pulled him toward Protection.

"Davy! You stop now!"

He heard Roberta yell to him. Her voice came from a distance and the darkness that he felt from Justin seemed to belong to someone else. His mind waged a fierce battle with itself. One part said to keep moving, the other told him to stop. Decided, he kept walking. Suddenly a hand gripped his arm and yanked him around almost sending him to the ground. His feet tangled and he had to grab a nearby tree to keep from falling.

Roberta jumped back for a moment when she saw the snarl on Davy's face. It didn't look like Davy at all. Just as quick as it appeared, it left. Davy stood there for a moment looking bewildered. Roberta felt goose bumps race down her arms as she watched the change course through him. They stood there looking at one another, red-faced and panting. Davy absently rubbed his arm where Roberta had grabbed him. Roberta stood tense, waiting to see what Davy would do next.

"What'd you do that for?" asked Davy.

"You wouldn't stop. I can't go any farther and Justin needs some more water. Look at him, he's all sweaty."

Davy blinked and then looked over his shoulder. He was surprised to see Justin there. Had he forgotten about him? Roberta took Justin off his back and laid him down. The urge to continue nagged him. Davy could feel the pull, like having an invisible rope tied around his waist, drawn by an unseen force. Davy paced nervously while Roberta held Justin and fed him water.

"You have a coat, Davy? Justin feels cold."

Davy took off his jacket. He was glad to have something to do to keep him busy. He wanted to bolt right up the trail and then off to the left, to the cave.

Roberta caught movement out of the corner of her eye and looked up to see a man walking down the trail toward them. He lifted his hand in a half wave as he passed by Davy. He smiled at Roberta, but when his eyes found Justin, the smile faltered. He continued by and turned twice more before he went around the bend. As soon as he moved out of sight, Roberta called to Davy.

"Davy! That man looked at us funny."

"So? People always look at me funny."

"I mean he stared at Justin. Maybe he knows. Do you think he came from Protection?"

"Adults don't know where Protection is, it's for kids. It doesn't matter now. We have to get going. You ready?"

"I'm tired. You have any of those snacks left? I'm hungry. My feet hurt, too."

"You can stay here if you want, Roberta! I have to get going. It's getting late." Davy's focus had returned to the cave. He felt an attraction he couldn't deny. He would go on without Roberta and not think twice. His earlier need to have her with him had dissipated like a fog in the summer sun.

"Okay, okay. I'm coming, but you're being a butthead."

***

Phil scanned both sides of the highway as he went up the canyon. He figured the three would stick out like a sore thumb. There weren't many people that walked up that road, especially double heavies like that. He traveled without his lights and slightly above the speed limit. He felt no particular urgency, plus it gave him time to swallow the last bits of his dog from the restaurant. He had calculated that at the most, he would spot the threesome about four miles up the canyon road, two miles past where he saw them last. He also kept his eye out for an abandoned car that may have been the reason for their march. When they didn't appear where he expected, he continued on up the hill. He assumed his estimate would put him plus or minus a mile, certainly no more than that. After two more miles up the road he pulled off into a ski resort parking lot. They probably caught a ride with a Good Samaritan, he thought.

He sat for a moment looking at his VDT unit, staring at the girl's picture. He closed his eyes until he saw the face again, tracking him as he went by; it was her all right. He pulled a U-turn and began rolling down the hill, slower this time, watching both sides. He reached for his radio to call in the sighting when his eyes went to the parking lot of the Sascone Peak Trail two miles below the empty ski resort. Without thinking it through, he pulled in and parked. He had no reason to believe they were hikers. They looked dead on their feet when he had seen them. Certainly, they were too fat to make a hike further than the refrigerator, yet they were miles from town. They didn't look dressed for hiking, either, and they also carried their kid, or a kid, if she was a runaway. Nothing close by could account for where they could have come from; no homes, no stores, no transportation. Wait! The trail did have a bus stop.

Maybe they had caught the bus back to town or rode it further up the mountain. He had no choice now. He picked up his radio to call in his location. As he talked to the dispatcher, he saw a man exit the trail and instead of going to his car, he walked right over to Phil.

"Can I help you?" Phil asked.

"Um, well, I don't know if it is anything or not. I just figured since you were here, I'd tell you."

"Go ahead, Sir."

"Well, about a mile up, I saw a man and woman with a boy, sitting along the trail. The boy didn't look so good. He had a big bump on his head and his arm was wrapped in a coat. Maybe he was asleep or something. I'm not sure, but the man and woman, well, they looked funny."

"Funny how?"

"Well, like not all there…in the head. Mentally handicapped or something. Not like they should have a boy with them, anyway."

"Would you know the woman if you saw her?"

"Maybe. I was walking by and I looked back a few times."

Phil sat back in his seat and turned the VDT toward the hiker so he could see the picture displayed there.

"Is that her?"

The hiker looked for only a few seconds and nodded his head.

"Yes sir, that's her all right."

Phil grabbed his radio again and contacted dispatch. He passed along the information from the civilian. He turned to the hiker once more.

"Did you see any weapons?"

"God no! They seemed harmless enough, it's just the boy didn't look well."

"Did it appear the girl was being held against her will?"

"No, she was sitting with the boy in her lap. She watched me the whole time, with barely a smile."

Phil asked and recorded the man's name and address for the report and questioned him one more time about how far up the trail he had seen them. Phil got out and locked his car. He looked over to the trailhead, hitched up his belt and started up the trail. The girl went up there, he was certain. So who was the guy with her and was he dangerous? And how did the kid fit into the picture?

He had only gone a few steps when he realized he had the wrong shoes for the task. They had no traction and weren't made for long hikes. If they saw him first, in his uniform, well, if they ran … Phil shook his head. If they ran? Those two couldn't outrun Grandma Moses. Still, it would be best if he walked quietly.

***

Davy started moving as Roberta tried to settle Justin on his back. Davy didn't act like Davy at all. She almost had run to keep up with him. She even lost him a few times around the corners in the trail. She could feel panic starting to rise at the thought of being lost or left behind.

She rounded a large boulder and saw Davy just standing there, looking through the woods toward the base of mountain. He appeared to be listening. Roberta followed his gaze. The rock face of the mountain poked up through the trees no more than a half mile away.

"What is it Davy?"

"Shhsss! I'm listening for the cry."

"What cry?"

"The one I heard last time. The one that led me to Protection."

"Where is it?"

"This way," he said and stepped off the trail.

The hiking became more difficult here, although the pace didn't get slower. They had to climb over downed trees and go around rock. Steep gullies forced Roberta to use her hands to help scale the steep walls and loose gravel caused her to slide going down the sides. Roberta watched as Davy walked almost a straight line through the woods. She worried about Justin riding on his back. Even though Davy held him tight, he still bounced around as Davy hiked uphill. Roberta watched as he walked straight into a tangle of bushes. Even she knew to walk around the tangle of fallen trees instead of trying to climb over them, but Davy didn't seem to notice. It took him so long to get through one tangle of bushes that Roberta met him on the other side as he came out. Normally, Roberta would have kidded him for being so slow, but when she saw that he didn't even notice and stared off into the distance behind her, she just let him pass.

"Davy! Let me carry Justin for a bit. He's getting scratched when you go through the bushes."

He turned on her quickly.

"No!"

Roberta stepped in front of him again.

"Davy! What's wrong? What's wrong with you?"

He tried to get by her but she held her ground in front of him.

"I have to get to Protection."

Davy could hear the children calling. He could almost see them, even though their images came incomplete and hazy. Even Mr. Harrington showed up in the picture in his mind. The pull, stronger and more urgent, felt like when Roberta pulled him down the aisle at the store. But something stood between him and Protection. Somewhere inside he knew Roberta blocked his progress and when he thought of her name, the angry feeling lessened and he could almost see her. His feelings fought a tug of war over his attention. He wanted to sit down in protest to the confusion in his mind. A bit of anger flowed through him. He hated not knowing what to do. He felt like throwing a tantrum right here and now.

Roberta stood quietly but firmly in front of him. Davy finally broke away from his distant stare long enough to focus on her, but the faraway look returned just as quickly. She started getting frightened. One of her friends at the house had done that before and then fell to the floor, shaking and wiggling around with foamy stuff coming from her mouth. If Davy did that now, Roberta knew she would just die from fright. Davy reached out and grabbed her arms, moving her to one side.

"We have to go. Protection's just up the hill."

TWENTY

The ulasiga was busy. It could feel its energy being expended as it continued to adjust to the Davy's mental state. It had connected with the man, a distance beyond what it had ever tried. Sometimes the reception came in clear and sometimes poor. Sometimes the Davy would shield his mind and other times it opened up. The ulasiga began to tire as it sped through signals sending them as fast and far as it could, always adjusting to the Davy's mental state. The meals came closer and now the ulasiga increased the power of its mind, unwilling to give the prey a chance to escape. The new memories to experience and food for a year, approached. The ulasiga could sense the small victim, the Justin, which moved with the bigger one. It also found strange new signals that the creature couldn't understand, funny patterns that made no sense; some originated from the Davy and some from the Justin. Sometimes they seemed to go back and forth to each other. The waves received from the Justin came in disjointed patterns making it even harder to decipher than the Davy. The ulasiga reached out. As the ulasiga pulled information from the Davy something else infiltrated its work. The ulasiga paused for a moment. It found another man coming with the Davy and the Justin. It made contact.

***

Roberta felt cold fingers touch her head inside. That and Davy grabbing her made her mad. She wanted to push him back like she had the woman beating him earlier. Instead, she mentally pushed away the fingers touching her head. She shoved them toward the mountain in the direction Davy was marching. She saw trees bend and a few birds fall to the ground but her anger kept her from caring. She turned back and allowed Davy to pass. She had to remind herself that Davy knew the way and that he had been asked to take Justin to Protection.

***

Out of nowhere, a huge wave of feedback burst through the ulasiga like an electric bolt. The shock didn't hurt, but the power and speed in which it moved surprised the creature. It hit like a tsunami; breaking the ulasiga's control. The predator backed off, trying to understand what had just happened. It had never experienced such an input. It redirected its memory searching for some previous event it could compare. The creature could find no code to match it. Satisfied that it wasn't injurious, it cautiously turned back to the Davy and latched on again. The difficult task continued and the ulasiga brought itself closer to the opening to better exert itself. Then the ulasiga once again found the signal that originated from the new man. It called itself Roberta. It disappeared as soon as it came. The ulasiga separated contact from the Davy to reach out to this Roberta. It came back, flickering like a light with a bad filament. The pattern appeared familiar, but not exactly. Three meals. Now the ulasiga turned up its reception another notch and the flow of information raced up and down the ulasiga's mind even faster. Three meals, three shows.

***

She decided to follow him as long as her boy, Justin, didn't get worse. She could feel the funny tickle that the thought gave her. My boy; an idea she had nursed for a couple of years; her and Davy and their own child. Then they would both be free of this thing that made them look stupid and made people think that they were dumb. They would look just like a family. She suddenly didn't want to let Justin go to Protection. They could take him to Davy's place and they could live there. She would stay home and take care of him. She could dress him and read to him or they could look at picture books together.

Her mind swam in this fantasy world as Davy continued smashing and crashing his way through everything in front of him. Then she remembered the man who had passed them on the trail. He didn't think they looked like a family. She could feel embarrassment and anger start to flood in. She also felt something else trying to sneak in. She didn't know where that feeling came from, but it felt cold, damp, and awful. She pushed it away along with the other thoughts. She dismissed the image of the man on the trail and went back to her fantasy.

Davy outpaced her now, a few steps at a time. Roberta didn't seem to notice. Somehow she knew Protection was just up the mountain and to the left a little.

Justin tried to hang on with what little strength he had, which wasn't much. Davy held him pretty tight, but the trip had become a little rougher. Justin knew that Protection lay up ahead. If Davy stopped and set him down, he'd still be able to get there. Justin felt a tickle in his scalp, like tiny fingers playing with his hair like his mother used to do. He wanted to reach up and scratch his head, but he was afraid to loosen his grip. He didn't feel well either. His stomach twisted in that strange way it did just before you threw up and one eye didn't want to focus. His mouth felt dry even after taking a drink, and one side of his face felt all puffy and numb, like when he had gone to the dentist. Unable to keep his eyes open, he slipped back into his dream as easily as pulling the covers over his head.

His dream took him back to Protection. He didn't see anyone there except Davy and the woman that had given him some water. She felt soft and Justin sat in her lap with his head against her chest. They both laughed their funny laugh and had their funny smiles. He felt warm and comfortable. He looked around Protection. He didn't see any other kids like Davy had said. In fact, he couldn't see much more than Davy. Now, he didn't see the girl because she sat behind him, holding him with her big soft arms. Then he could feel her tickling his head. He wanted to reach up and push her hand away. It tickled too much. But his arms wouldn't move. They felt too heavy to lift, so he left them limp at his side and giggled at the feeling.

***

Davy hardly noticed the sharp pain in his side and his hammering heart. He focused everything on getting to Protection. He had to get there. He had to get there now. It wasn't far. It sat just around the next corner and although he couldn't stop if he wanted, he knew that when he saw the entrance his head would just explode. The images of Mr. Harrington and the two children cleared, but they flickered like the lights in the window of the grocery store where he worked. The images hummed like them, too. He wanted to reach up and cover his ears to block it out but he had to hold Justin. Sweat ran into his eyes and blurred his vision. He was glad he didn't need to see to find his way.

He worked his way around the rock outcropping and saw it, just a small black hole in the side of the mountain. For some reason Davy had expected a big house with double doors and a sign out front with Protection in capital letters. He had forgotten. With the cave in sight, the pull had lessened and Davy set Justin down. He wanted to go inside and find Mr. Harrington. He wanted to know if Protection had a doctor for Justin. Roberta came puffing up behind him. Before Davy could walk into the little cave she grabbed him.

"Davy! Can't we keep Justin?"

"Huh? Do what?"

"Keep Justin. We could take care of him. He doesn't need to go to that place."

"What place?"

"Davy! Are you listening?"

Davy alternated between Roberta and the cave entrance without seeing either. His mind had become a jumbled tangle of thought without the insistent pull that had driven him this far. Different feelings seemed to flow into his head without invitation, all the while trying to catch his breath from the hike. He tried to remember what to do next. He snapped out of it when a pinecone bounced off his head. He turned back toward Roberta who giggled.

"Davy! Wake up, you dope."

Davy tried to smile, but he didn't have the energy to manufacture one. He felt strange. His mind had been full of things, things he didn't understand, and then all of the strange things left. He felt empty. Slowly his mind began to settle and he could think clearly for the first time in hours.

"I'm sorry, Roberta. I was thinking of something else. What'd you say?"

"I said we could keep Justin. We could take care of him better then anybody."

Davy looked at Justin sleeping quietly in Roberta's lap and then he looked at Roberta's face. Her eyes sparkled and she smiled that secret smile Davy often saw on mothers' faces in the store when they looked at their children. He had never thought about what Roberta said but he thought about it now. He could feel those feelings well up inside again. The ones he got when he looked into the eyes of happy children. He pictured them all at his apartment; happy Justin with bright eyes and a big smile. He could imagine them all together in the park. He could push both Justin and Roberta on the swings. Mothers at the park would smile at the happy threesome instead of the cold stare he usually got alone. The three of them could walk the trails together. He could show them all the different colors. Maybe they could.

***

Phil moved quickly and silently up the trail. It wasn't long before he began huffing like a smoker on a treadmill. He could feel his calf muscles protesting the unscheduled work. Phil kept up a rigorous fitness schedule because it was another rule; stay in better shape than your opponent. He ran three miles every day and worked out in the gym as often as he could, but walking up a fairly steep incline at a rapid pace in bad shoes was a whole different ballgame. He wished he'd brought some water. He looked at his watch and saw he had been hiking for fifteen minutes. They shouldn't be too far ahead.

He wondered what drove him so hard. If the description given by the man down there at the trailhead was correct, the girl should be fine. Maybe the kid pushed his cop button. The hiker had said he didn't look good and had a lump on his head. More likely the odd picture bothered him. A kid, maybe injured, a missing girl, mentally slow, and an unknown guy, all grouped together, none of them smiling, but not acting scared made a very strange collage. None of it made sense and that irritated his senses. Phil realized that his comfort zone lay in knowing what he faced. Even when he took on armed felons, at least he knew the bad guys from the good. He found more tension in a traffic stop than in a high-speed chase. You never knew what the driver in a stopped car could do.

He paused for a minute to catch his breath and check in on his radio. They had sent some Park Rangers and two more units to assist. What a relief. Park Rangers would have the right shoes at least.

"There's no way they'll be here before I find the three of them," Phil said to the empty woods. He even began to practice the approach he would use; hand on weapon to be safe, a smile to disarm the fear at seeing a cop, say yes ma'am, no sir, be calm, quiet and polite, watch for others that may be hiding in the woods, put your back in a safe place. He started up the trail again.

He began to think he had passed the place where they should have been if they hadn't moved. Again the whys began to nag him. Why would they go up the trail? He knew of nothing up there but the end. Without knowing why, he veered off the trail and went into the woods. He stopped and looked around. He saw only trees, bushes, and rocks, but he felt an urge to continue through the woods. He didn't know why. Instead, he turned back and continued up the slope following the trail. They had to be within two miles and the three couldn't go as fast as he could. He would catch them in fifteen minutes for sure. He wiped the sweat from his forehead and cursed the blister forming on his ankle from his dress shoes.

Ten minutes later, Phil thought he heard voices. He immediately went into a crouch. He turned his radio down so an unexpected call wouldn't alert them to his presence. He unsnapped the hold down strap on his holster and pulled the gun half way out so it wouldn't hang up on anything. He quickly scanned the surrounding forest for any movement and looked back down the trail for anyone trying to sneak up behind him. When he realized how he acted, he straightened back up and took a deep breath. These were just people, lost, crazy, or running. They weren't a gang of murderous thieves. Still, his hand remained on his gun. The voices got louder. They came down the trail toward him. He moved to the side to better shield himself from the trail. They wouldn't see him till they rounded the corner twenty feet away. He saw a flicker of red through the woods and then a spot of yellow. His mind flashed back to when he first saw them as he drove down the hill toward the city. Hadn't the trio been wearing red and yellow? Again, he found himself crouched and tense.

Finally, the owners of the voices rounded the corner. He saw two kids, no more than eighteen, hiking down the trail; some guy and his girlfriend, no doubt. They weren't the ones he wanted. They weighed about half of the two. They stopped their jabbering in mid-sentence when they saw him, surprised by seeing a State Trooper in full uniform on the trail. Phil let his gun slide back in the holster and wiped his sweaty palm on his pant leg. He stood up straight from the stance he had taken and put a smile on his face. He wasn't quick enough, though. He could see the color drain from the two teens faces. They must have thought they had walked into the middle of a firefight.

"I'm sorry," Phil said. "I didn't mean to scare you."

The two stood stone still and stared as they paled even further.

"You two pass anybody on the trail?"

"Huh?"

"Did you see anyone else on the trail? A man with a kid and a girl?"

The girl finally seemed to comprehend what he said and shook her head.

Phil had expected them to say that his quarry was just ahead. His surprise at the answer she had given him led him to repeat the question.

"You didn't see anyone?"

"Sure. There're two guys back there," the boy said. He hitched his thumb back over his shoulder.

"What do they look like?"

"Young. Rock climbers, I guess. They had a bunch of rope and climbing gear and stuff, ya know, like those metal things."

"That's it? Nobody else?"

"No, sir."

Phil looked at them carefully, not really believing them. They were hiding something. Then it occurred to him. They probably had a joint or two on them. That's why they acted so scared. Kids!

"Okay, thanks," he said.

The two moved past and Phil turned back toward them. "Hey!"

They stopped and turned back toward Phil, still pale and nervous.

"There'll be Park Rangers and police at the trailhead. I'd lose the pot."

Without looking at their reaction, Phil turned and looked back up the trail. Decision time. Continue up or head back down.

Phil continued up the trail. He didn't know why, but what else could he do? Where could they have gone? Off trail! Where else? He began to look for signs where they may have gone into the woods or took a side trail. The idea that he should wait for the Rangers crossed his mind causing him to pause. Might as well wait for the professionals, he thought. He turned around and started back. Until the Rangers showed up, he would look for signs on his way to his car.

TWENTY-ONE

The ulasiga quit, exhausted. It needed a rest. Never had the creature had to use so much energy trying to capture a meal. Now that his prey, the Davy, remained at the entrance, it could ease back some effort for a moment, ready to reapply it should he begin to move away. The real work hadn't started. It had been surprised to find the Roberta instead of just the Davy and the Justin. It encountered unexpected problems, too. The Davy wasn't difficult because of the memories implanted during the first meeting. The Justin didn't respond as the other. Unlike the patterns of the Davy, his brain waves constantly changed and some places became altogether impenetrable. The shifting waves had no basic pattern to copy and trying to extract images from such a distance strained the ability of the ulasiga. Even the little one's heart and breathing came in irregular patterns. It may be difficult to bring it down slow enough to extract the memories before they faded with death. Although the ulasiga wanted the memories, it could be satisfied with the Davy as long as it could get him to bring the small man into the deep cave.

The Roberta presented the biggest problem. And the least understood. It had been totally beyond the ulasiga. At one point the ulasiga had released the Davy and the Justin, focusing all of its power on the Roberta. It had almost been able to connect and then somehow the touch it had sent all came back in a giant reverberation, much like the earlier one. It had been unexpected and the resultant energy burst shocked the creature.

Just before the short circuit, it felt the presence of a fourth. Then the presence had disappeared. It had only taken a second for the creature to recover and lightly reconnect to the Davy and the Justin. It had felt the Roberta follow along without its help, so it decided to not be greedy and just concentrate on the two. Now that all three stood just outside, it felt it could bring them all in.

But first it wanted to secure its food supply so it would have to get the Davy to bring the Justin one in close enough. Once both moved into the darkness, it would bring them both down to a comatose state. With luck, it could take the memories and run them. After the memories, the ulasiga would send the Davy back for more. The Roberta he would draw inside and that one, too, would go down and provide a show for the ulasiga. Once the show ended it could begin the process of dissolving the bodies and transferring the liquid to storage deep below. It would take months to move all the food to the lair, but it would feed the ulasiga for years. Rested and decided, the ulasiga went back to work.

***

Phil stopped where he had turned into the woods earlier. He looked into the forest of pine and birch, boulders and weeds. Phil felt that sixth sense he used so often. A feeling told him they had gone into the woods. Perhaps he should hike that direction for just a little ways to see if he could find any signs the trio had gone that way. He wiggled his toes in his shoes and moved his ankles back and forth as he peered into the woods. He winced when he felt the sting of raw flesh on his ankle touch the side of his shoe. Maybe just a few feet, he thought. Phil slowly made his way over a downed tree and past a large boulder. About fifty feet in, he stopped. He closed his eyes and searched for that same feeling that had stopped him cold on the trail. He twisted a little right and then a bit to the left. It reminded him of the old TV antennas that had to be moved to pick up the best reception. Nothing. He opened his eyes and began looking around for more obvious signs. Maybe they had left a candy wrapper or cellophane from a HoHo. A big trio should leave signs everywhere. As he went to turn back, he saw the line of busted limbs through a dead fall. He walked over to it and examined it closely. It looked fresh. Could it have been a deer? An elk? It went directly through leaving broken branches. The destruction looked more like a bear … or a fat man. Phil examined several of the breaks looking for hair. If it had been an animal, he should see hair rubbed off on the breaks. He saw none. He moved to the other side of the dead tree and put his back to the path he had found. He walked away from it in a straight line until he came to another blow over and, again, saw where something heavy had crashed through. This time he saw a yellow thread hanging from one of the stubs from a broken branch. Whoever made the trail did it as the crow flies. He couldn't see any deviation from the line. Now Phil lined himself up with the trail being carved through the woods and looked ahead as far as he could. This time he felt something. At first he dismissed it as overactive input or wishful thinking. He had been hunting this trio down since noon and it was now two thirty. He had walked what seemed like miles at high speed in bad shoes. His alert level had been dialed up to full for two and a half continuous hours.

A lot of what he saw, or felt, he credited to self-induced hallucinations; something he had seen and experienced before. He knew he had to fight these feelings. It caused innocent people to get shot. He stopped and let out a few pent up breaths. He walked himself slowly through his past actions making sure he understood the goal. The little boy had to come first. He felt uncomfortable with the thought that the child may be hurt and in the care of one slow girl and an unknown man. Add to it the fact that he wasn't sure about what lay ahead, it also made his heart pump a little harder. Could the man be some drifter that kidnapped the boy and lured in the girl? How retarded was she, he wondered? Could this guy get her to come along willingly, then bring her to the woods? For what? Rape? Murder? Could be. Phil turned back toward the direction the trail led. Again, he closed his eyes and tried to feel the lure. He spun in circles until he didn't know which way he faced. Then twisting slightly left and right, he found the signal. He opened his eyes and saw that he stared right down the line he'd been following. No mistake, instinct guided him. He began to walk the line.

***

Davy turned back toward the cave entrance and looked at it for a long time. Could this be Protection? How? Then he felt the touch again. It started as a whisper, no more than a feathery touch in his mind. It called to him. He searched out the source with his own mind trying to identify it as Mr. Harrington or one of the children. He looked at Justin who now lay in Roberta's lap. He found what little feelings escaped from Justin wasn't what called to him now.

"I have to take Justin in to Mr. Harrington. You wait here."

"Take him where?" Roberta asked looking around.

"To Protection," Davy said.

"Where's it at? How much farther?" she asked.

"We're here. I have to take him inside the cave. It's in there," he said pointing.

Roberta looked to where he pointed and then looked back at him. "You're crazy, Davy. That's just a hole. There's no house or people in there."

"Yes there is. I have to take him. I have to get him to Mr. Harrington."

"No. Leave Justin here. Go find the doctor and bring him back. I'll take care of him."

"I have to take him," Davy said looking back and forth between Roberta and the cave entrance.

"No you don't, Davy! He needs to rest a moment."

Davy looked at Roberta, her face set in that stubborn way he knew so well. He glanced over his shoulder and then back at her. Unable to wait anymore, he turned toward the cave.

"You're coming back aren't you?"

"Of course. I'll just find Mr. Harrington and see about a doctor."

Roberta looked down into Justin's face. He not only looked pale and sweaty, but one side of his face looked different from the other. The knot had gone down some, but now it looked like his whole head was swelling.

"Hurry!" she told him.

Davy took a deep breath and entered the main cave where he had waited out the rainstorm. He strained to see deeper inside but couldn't penetrate the dark. He stepped carefully through the blackness toward the back near the smaller entrance, steered by that same feeling that had brought him this far. He got down on his knees and put his head by the hole. He tried to feel the presence of the children. Something else in there called to him, drawing him closer and urging him inside, it wasn't them. The thing in his head reminded him of the black circle and Davy shivered. He almost pulled back out as the darkness enveloped him. Instead, he sent a wave of warmth back in hoping that the children inside would respond.

He looked back into the hole and saw blackness so deep he could have had his eyes closed tight, blacker than the closet. He swallowed his fear and wiggled through.

"Mr. Harrington? Mr. Harrington? You in here?"

Davy heard his words die without an echo.

The tingling inside came on stronger so Davy crawled deeper into the opening. The lack of light and the smallness of the cave made him nervous. How could that big house fit in here and where was it? They should have at least had lights on in the windows. Then weariness gripped him and he found he didn't have the strength to crawl. It had been a long walk and a long day. He laid his head down on his arms and closed his eyes.

***

Roberta watched as Davy moved toward the opening. He walked slow and stiff like a robot or one of those TV monsters she saw on Saturday night. He turned and disappeared into the black opening.

Roberta now sat alone with Justin. She looked down at him and began talking to him as she stroked his face and hair.

"It's okay. You rest. Davy is going to find a doctor for you and then we'll get you fixed up. Maybe you can stay with us and we will take care of you, feed you and all that stuff," she said. She spoke as much to calm her own fears as to soothe the boy. It hadn't even been a minute and she already wondered what took Davy so long. Roberta looked around expecting to see some wild animal stalking up behind her. She pulled Davy's backpack closer and opened it to get Justin some more water. She found the bottle under an apple and a small first aid kit. She also found a flashlight. Her eyes drifted to the cave and then down at the flashlight. When she turned it on, she winced as the bright light hit her eyes. She turned it off and put it back where she found it. She adjusted Davy's windbreaker over Justin, covering him as much as possible, carefully placing his head on the knapsack for a pillow. Roberta, again, looked at the cave entrance where Davy had gone and back at the flashlight. She sat there, momentarily held in place by indecision. She wanted to find Davy and see what held him up, but she didn't want to leave Justin lying there alone. What about the wild animals that inhabited these woods, she wondered? What if she walked away and a lion carried him off? Maybe she could stay within sight of Justin. She just wanted to take a quick peek inside and see where Davy went. She still didn't understand how a house and people could be inside.

***

The ulasiga didn't wait for the Davy to make it all the way to the back. As soon as his bulk blocked out all the light, the ulasiga put him down. It rebuilt the house and children for the Davy and then caused him to wake to see it. The ulasiga scrambled to rearrange everything rejected by the Davy's mind until it felt the waves smooth out. The ulasiga halted when it found the man's memory had changed from the first time. Initially, the ulasiga had wanted to put the big man to sleep and then bring in the child, but found itself unable to work the mind of the little one. It didn't know why it couldn't connect with the small one. Instead, the ulasiga would have to use the big one to bring the meal inside where it could reach. The third man, the one the ulasiga couldn't reach at all may escape. There was nothing the creature could do about it.

The ulasiga manipulated Davy's mind like a puppeteer, pulling strings of memory and reason to get him to do what needed to be done.

First, it could feel the need for the Mr. Harrington's image, so it produced it. It then found the voice and found the answers to the questions not yet asked. The ulasiga didn't understand any of the language, it only knew that intertwining the pattern and keeping it smooth got results. It could feel the rightness in its actions.

Davy woke back inside Protection. At first the children had the wrong hair … maybe. Then the looks; they weren't smiling, and then they were. Davy said hi and sent them a tickle. They didn't seem to notice, but neither did Davy, who looked for Mr. Harrington. Then Mr. Harrington appeared out of thin air. Davy blinked as if he saw a ghost.

"Is that you, Mr. Harrington?"

"Of course, Davy. Who'd you expect?" he said with a smile.

Davy hesitated for a moment, not as sure. What he saw didn't match what had appeared before. The first time he had seen Protection it had been right, everything; the children, Mr. Harrington, Protection. Now it just felt different, unreal, dreamlike.

"I see you brought us a child," Mr. Harrington said.

"Yes, sir. He's hurt though and he needs a doctor. Is there one here?"

"A doctor? Uh, sure, Davy. We have everything here. It's Protection. Everything a child needs, just like at the store."

"He looks pretty bad. He has a bump on his head and he sleeps all the time. He's talking funny. You sure you can fix him?"

For just a moment Mr. Harrington wavered. His image shimmered like the road on a hot summer day. Mr. Harrington became solid again.

"Bring him in to me Davy so I can take care of him. Bring him all the way in and come in yourself. Stay awhile."

***

Roberta glanced back behind Justin, almost expecting to see a group of lions sneaking through the forest toward him.

"Don't worry. I'll be right back," she called back to Justin.

She walked toward the entrance, alternating between looking at Justin and looking at the dark hole in the rock. As she got closer, she began to lose some of her resolve.

"Davy! Davy! Answer me!" she yelled at the darkness.

She turned on the flashlight and pointed it at the interior. It made no change in the dark hole in front of her. The brightness of the day washed away the beam of light. She didn't see Davy anywhere from where she stood. She took another step closer to the entrance and swept the light back and forth. She could see a pale yellow on the sides of the wall but nothing deeper inside. Still several feet away from the opening, she took another tentative step toward the black interior. Movement from the shadows sent shivers through her. Goosebumps appeared immediately on her arms as she imagined a tiger or even a zombie coming from inside to attack. She turned to run and realized that Justin lay just a few feet away, helpless. She would have to fend off the monster to save him. She turned back to face it, ready to push it away. Then she realized it was Davy and she relaxed her hand that had raised the flashlight in defense. She smiled and tried to tell him he had scared her but Davy acted funny. He walked past her without a look and went directly to where Justin lay on the grass. Davy bent over and picked him up.

"Do they have a doctor?" Roberta asked.

Davy said nothing as he moved back toward the entrance. Roberta grabbed his arm.

"Davy! Do they have a doctor? Can we keep him?"

She suddenly started to panic when Davy didn't reply. He never even looked at her. He pulled free from her grasp and continued toward the mouth of the cave. This time Roberta ran around in front of him, blocking his path.

"Davy! What's the matter? Are you all right?"

Without a word, Davy moved around her and entered the dark. Roberta sat heavily and began to cry.

TWENTY-TWO

Phil was getting closer to the trio. He knew it. He looked back along the path he had taken through the trees. He couldn't see the brown dirt that defined the Sascone Peak trail. He had gone a half, maybe even a mile. The hiking had become harder. He had to work his way through fallen trees to keep from losing the path, his shoes slipping often on the smooth bark as he climbed over limbs. He wanted to skirt the steep gullies and all the other obstacles that lay in the direction of the fresh breaks, but he thought he might lose the trail. The path led upward toward the stone face of the mountain. What he searched for must lie around the corner of a large stone outcropping just in front of him.

Unwilling to surprise his quarry while all out of breath, he leaned against a large boulder and settled himself. He pulled out his gun, a Glock 23, and slid a round into the chamber. He re-holstered the gun, and snapped the strap back in place. He felt his belt making sure he still had everything; handcuffs, mace, extra clips, his duty flashlight. He began moving forward again, now trying to quiet his steps. He wanted surprise on his side.

Phil made it to the edge of a high rock outcropping that blocked his view of what lay ahead. He kept his back up against the rough granite of the sheer cliff. He pulled his gun and held it in both hands, combat style. He stood silently, listening, for a moment, but all he heard was the sighing of the wind through the trees. Slowly, he inched his way around the rock, continually sweeping the surrounding area for movement. Finally, he saw some color. He slipped behind some cover to prepare himself for the confrontation. He took a deep breath, held it for a second, and then slowly exhaled. He stepped back into the open and quickly assessed the area. Only one person sat there and she wore a red jacket. She had her back to him. He slowly moved toward the girl. If his memory served him, the girl on the road wore a red jacket. Then he heard the girl crying, her back shaking as she sobbed. Phil checked out the area one more time looking for anyone else.

"Miss? Are you all right?" he called out to her.

Roberta felt jagged waves of electricity run through her when she heard the voice. Her tears cut off abruptly and she stiffened, afraid to turn around.

Phil saw her reaction to his words and knew she had heard him, but she didn't turn to acknowledge him. He felt his adrenalin start to flow and he shook it off. This was just a young girl, but where were the others? He tried again.

"Miss, don't be scared. Nobody's going to hurt you. Are you okay? Is everything okay?"

Slowly, Roberta turned to see who was speaking. The gun in his hand didn't register, but the uniform did. At first she was relieved to see a policeman, but then she remembered what Davy had said. He wanted to arrest her for leaving without a pass. Now they would send her to jail. And Davy, too!

"Leave us alone!"

Phil quickly checked the area again. He didn't see anyone. He could still feel that little tickle of danger. He looked back at the girl. Sure enough, she matched the one on the flyer, the missing girl. He could see the recognizable appearance of a child with Down syndrome. She had big eyes and a round face, with the straight black hair. He could hear it in her voice, too, but she wasn't retarded. She knew he was a cop, but instead of relief, she looked scared. He spoke again, using the softest voice he could produce. He felt exposed, like being in the middle of a mine field.

"I'm not going to hurt you, Miss. Where are your friends, the big one and the little boy? Are they okay?"

Roberta recoiled. She would lose Justin either way. Why did she always have to lose? Why did everyone think she was so stupid? She could remember Betty laughing at her and calling her a dummy. She could remember spending hours trying to remember simple things like noodles, the spaghetti things. She had held Justin and taken care of him without hurting him. She had given him water and food and he didn't choke or die. Even when she did good nobody noticed and now the police, instead of helping, came to make sure she would never have her own baby. They would lock her up and Davy, too. They would never see each other again. She started to get mad. She would give him one more chance to just leave or she would push him away, just like that mean woman that hit Davy, except this time she would to push hard!

"Go away! Leave us alone! We didn't do anything wrong!"

Phil could see the anger building in the girl. He might have trouble restraining her if she fought, so it was best to keep the situation calm. He re-holstered his weapon. He put both hands out so she could see he meant no harm. He put on his best smile and eased his voice down another notch. He could feel the air thicken between him and the girl, some weird invisible wall seemed to keep him from moving closer. He searched for the right words to calm her down while trying to figure out why he felt a wind on such a still day.

"I know. It's just your friends are worried about you because they didn't know where you went. The little boy may be hurt. I want to see if I can help. Where is he?"

Roberta paused. Justin did need help. Davy didn't say if he found a doctor at Protection. But what if the policeman lied and just wanted to arrest Davy. Mr. Harrington would help wouldn't he? Roberta felt dizzy trying to think about all the possibilities. She wished she had Davy here to help her decide. Maybe she could go ask him first. Instead she blurted out, "They're at Protection."

Phil thought he misunderstood. It sounded like she said protection. The girl must be mixed up? Had she left them behind somewhere?

"Excuse me?"

"They're at Protection. They're safe now with Mr. Harrington and the other kids."

"Mr. Harrington? Other kids? Where's this Protection? Where are they?"

"It's in there," she said pointing over her shoulder. "But you can't go there. It's just for kids that have been hurt by their mommies and daddies."

Phil felt really baffled now. He looked to where she pointed and saw only shadow. His radio crackled and he heard the backup calling him.

"Trooper Nine, we're at the trail. Where's the turn off?"

He reached down and quickly turned it off but he was too late. He saw all the gains he had made with the girl vanish. He watched as her face went from confusion to fear and back to anger. He searched desperately for the words he could say to defuse the situation, even if he didn't understand. He felt that invisible wall thicken. His sixth sense told him not to approach the girl. Then he felt the wall of air start pushing him backward. It hit him thick and insistent. Phil's mind reeled with shock. Something was forcing him back, something like a soft but insistent hand. It lifted him from the ground and carried him backward. He waved his arms helplessly as the ground got farther away and the speed of his flight increased. His ride ended suddenly when his back hit the rock face of the cliff. The mountain side dimmed and he felt himself falling.

Roberta watched the policeman fly backwards. When she saw how high and how fast he flew, her anger turned back to fear. She pulled back some just before he hit, crumpled, and landed in a heap. She wanted to rush to his side and tell him she was sorry. She wanted to see if he needed help, but Justin came first.

***

Davy carried Justin as far as the small entrance to the deeper cave. He laid him down on the floor almost grateful that he couldn't see his face. He wiggled through the still too-small entrance, turned and reached out, feeling for Justin. He found an arm and began pulling him inside. He tried not to pull too hard. He didn't want to hurt him. Davy's mind flooded with a thousand thoughts, directions, and feelings. He felt scared at the massive input. He found that so much flew around inside that he couldn't feel Justin at all. He sent him a touch of warmth and a tickle just in case. All the time he kept calling for Mr. Harrington to bring a doctor.

A small moan escaping from the boy's still body scared him. He thought maybe he had pulled a little too hard. He sat turned in an awkward position in the cave and he found his strength waning. To add to all the difficulties, he couldn't see. He remembered his flashlight in his backpack. That thought brought a sudden sharp pain in his head. He stopped pulling and held both sides of his head, covering his ears. He pressed on his temples hoping it would make the pain go away. When it did, he fainted.

***

The ulasiga continued to quickly generate overlays of the prey's thought patterns. The image of a bright light suddenly came to the ulasiga and it contracted for protection, releasing all its mental control. It shrunk back deeper into the crevice it had pooled into before it realized the Davy had generated the picture and it wasn't really light at all. The involuntary contraction and sudden removal of control caused the man to crumple.

The ulasiga was inexperienced at manipulating such massive control and had been over compensating to keep from losing its free meal. It had to draw the Davy in and then get him to drag the Justin along, but it became taxing work. The ulasiga could feel the drain at the same time another pattern interrupted the flow. The fourth, a Phil, had come back into range.

The creature felt the big man Davy wake, but now his patterns had changed. They had become scattered, flipping from one to another quicker than the ulasiga could respond and the small one could not be penetrated. The ulasiga tried to keep the image it had created of the other children it found inside the big man, but for some unknown reason his prey wasn't accepting those images anymore. It had used those images available in the memory of the man without success. It tried focusing on the one called Mr. Harrington. The Davy seemed to respond best to that pattern, but now the big man fought that image, too.

The ulasiga turned for a moment to the two men outside the entrance. It found one difficult to connect with and the other too far away. The creature tested the darkness in the small cavern and found too much light. It could feel heat from what little entered through the hole.

Instead of reaching back out and regaining control, the ulasiga stopped. The ulasiga needed to rest and re-evaluate its position.

***

Davy slowly came to. He could feel the cool of the dirt floor of the small cave. At first he thought he had gone blind. He shook his head. The lack of sight didn't register right away as he searched his brain for a foreign input. Something had been in there. He could feel empty places and a certain serenity in the new quiet. Davy thought he was on his back staring straight up at the roof of the interior cave. Even with his eyes wide open he couldn't see anything. He waved his hand in front of his face and he couldn't see it either. He turned his head and could barely make out a dark shadow from the small opening where Justin lay half in and half out of the hole. He turned his head the other direction to find Protection but he saw nothing but blackness. Davy wondered for a moment how he had ended up inside the cave. He thought back as far as he could. He only remembered the park, where he and Roberta shared a laugh and then only tiny snatches since then.

Was Roberta still with him or had he left her behind? A shiver ran through him. Once more he wondered what happened to Mr. Harrington? Protection? Justin needed some help. He had to go and check on Roberta and help her if she needed him. He had brought her into this.

He had imagined carrying Justin in his arms as he climbed the steps into Protection like a hero. He had imagined Mr. Harrington with a smile and the children all gathering around to see the new addition. And he had pictured Roberta watching, clapping her hands. It turned out nothing like that. He shivered, cold and frightened. He sat in the darkest place he had ever been and the fear had taken over. Worst of all, he felt alone. Panic started to nip at the edges of his mind and he crawled quickly toward the hole. He wanted to shove Justin out of the way and get out. He needed air and he wanted to see light. He crawled quickly on his hands and knees, feeling but ignoring the stones cutting into his knees. Air! He couldn't breathe! He needed air! He got to the entrance and felt Justin's head and arm. He began to push him out of the hole.

He hesitated when he felt the first touch lightly enter him and settle in his head. Before he could think about it, what it was, or where it came from, he heard a sound. It was sobbing, like a child, but then he recognized it, not from children, but from his childhood, familiar and frightening. Unable to help himself, he rolled back into a sitting position. Exhaustion overwhelmed him, forcing him to drop his head onto his knees. He didn't know if his eyes closed or not and he really didn't care. Davy felt so tired, both mentally and physically. He wanted to lie down and sleep for a hundred years.

His eyes opened, or did they? He stood back inside Protection, but with no children, no toys, no furniture, just Mr. Harrington, maybe. He looked a lot like Mr. Harrington and Davy couldn't pinpoint the difference, he just knew it wasn't exactly him.

"Mr. Harrington?"

"Davy."

"Mr. Harrington, what is going on? Nothing seems to work. Nothing is right. I'm so tired."

"Bring the little man in and you both can rest here on the couch."

Mr. Harrington pointed to the empty spot behind him and a big overstuffed couch appeared. It looked exactly like the one Davy imagined when he heard Mr. Harrington say couch. It looked so comfortable, so nice. He could hold Justin in his arms and they could sleep. He turned back toward Justin and the scene followed him. Davy felt too tired to fight the inconsistencies. The big fat cushions! The large pillows! He patted his hand around blindly until he found an arm. He began to slowly pull the boy through the hole.

TWENTY-THREE

Roberta sat watching the body of the policeman. At first she expected him to get back up and when he didn't, she thought maybe she killed him. A wave of jumbled emotions crashed over her. She got to her feet and staggered toward the cave entrance. She stood in the valley between two fears, the darkness and unknown ahead and the dead policeman and prison behind. She needed Davy. He would know what to do. She moved into the cave and was swallowed immediately by darkness. She went as far as she could see and stopped, waiting for her eyes to adjust. She remembered the flashlight in Davy's backpack and turned to retrieve it. Already the light coming in from outside the opening caused her to squint. She kept her eyes on the still form of the man beside the rock face as she moved slowly to Davy's backpack. She fumbled trying to open it without looking. The policeman groaned and moved just a bit. Roberta dropped the bag with the light still inside and ran back to the cave. She knew she wouldn't go back out there without Davy. She crawled deeper into the cave.

"Davy!"

She listened for his reply. Nothing.

She moved a little farther in, holding her hands in front of her, feeling her way blindly.

"Davy! Please! Davy! Answer me!"

She listened. The rattle of her breath masked all other sounds. She took a deep breath and held it. There! A sound! A small scraping noise came from in front of her near the floor and a few feet forward. She slowly eased a little further into the cave while waving her hands in front of her. When she felt nothing, she took a small step forward. She dropped down to her knees and brushed around the dirt floor in front of her. She continued to crawl forward feeling her way when her hand made contact with Justin's leg. The minute she touched it, it pulled forward out of her grasp. The sudden movement scared her and she instinctively pulled back. Then, as she realized what she had touched, she forced herself to reach out and grab the leg. This time she held on tight.

"Davy! Where are you?" she yelled.

Nothing. She kept her grip while walking her hands up the boy's thin body until she felt the opening to the interior cave at the boy's knees. Justin was almost all the way through. Roberta peered into the opening and saw nothing.

"Davy! It's me, Roberta! Say something."

When Davy didn't answer, Roberta became frightened. What if it wasn't Davy pulling Justin through? What if some monster hid in there? There wasn't any place called Protection inside that hole! Roberta grabbed both legs and pulled. Justin didn't move. She saw an image of her pulling him in two, hurting him even more so she eased back a little.

"Davy. Help," she cried, only softer now. More tears began to form in her eyes as she felt the hopelessness.

Then she felt a tickle in her head. Not really a tickle. More like an unexpected spider web, the kind that you didn't see but felt when it touched you. Sure it tickled, but it was frightening, scary, yucky, and you always knew the spider had landed on you. Goosebumps formed on her arms as the feeling covered more of her scalp, but from the inside. Then it felt like hands with fingers playing over her brains, trying to read like the blind kids did, their fingers lightly touching and then retreating and touching again. Then she felt like she couldn't breathe. Some dark spider had crawled inside her head touching her. Suddenly she remembered! She remembered everything! Something in those fingers had unlocked a treasure chest of memories. She remembered her mother in detail, the hugs and kisses. She remembered where she lived now and all of the people in the house. She knew her room was the third door on the left. Spaghetti! The fingers began to touch her even faster, tapping more of her mind. She remembered the class about inappropriate touching. Her fear turned to anger. She pushed the hands away, hard, mentally slapping them, hoping it would sting! She felt Justin slide a few inches toward her as she pulled on his leg. She took advantage of the moment and slid him all the way out of the hole.

***

The ulasiga lay stunned. All of its control, all of its victims, lost. It hadn't seen the reverberation coming back from its probe on the Roberta, the one trying to steal its food. The ulasiga had only been looking for an opening to the brain patterns when suddenly millions of tiny sparkling memories filled its being. The images showed clear and fresh like they had been hidden for years, untouched, unsullied by use. The input was wonderful for the ulasiga and it was so overwhelmed by visions that it didn't notice the wave; huge, jagged, a high speed energy pulse of enormous size following behind until it was too late. First, it tried to stop it, then dissipate it, but it came too fast. When the surge hit the ulasiga's core, it disrupted the creature's hold. The ulasiga had never been the receiver of a forced thought. It was a sender that monitored and adjusted what it pulled from the victims. What hit it had been almost like a physical punch. The memories that it watched before the feedback had been a treat but the huge pulse following it was punishing. It took several seconds for the creature to recover. It shook off the effects and tried to reestablish control of the Davy, the only one of the three that the ulasiga could easily control.

It could feel the Justin being pulled into the light by the Roberta, the one that had initiated the reverberation that had slammed into its brain. The ulasiga refocused on the only meal it had within its grasp. It tried to command the Davy to retrieve the child but got no response. The Davy had passed out.

***

Roberta managed to drag Justin the rest of the way out of the small hole and pulled him into her lap. She held him and rocked him in the dark. Feeling his face, she managed to brush the hair out of his eyes and the dirt from his cheeks. He felt lifeless in her arms. Roberta just knew he had died and she began to cry. She kissed his cold cheek as big fat tears ran from her eyes. She held him as she felt her way back toward the entrance of the cave, all the time calling his name. When she reached the light, she stood with him in her arms and slowly made her way back toward the entrance.

***

Phil blinked twice trying to get his eyes to focus. Finally, he could make out branches of a tree silhouetted against the blue sky. His head throbbed and felt like it had grown three sizes too big. He quickly checked for his gun, then he reached for his radio. It was shattered by his hip hitting the rock wall. Using his hands for support, Phil forced himself into a sitting position, stopping for a moment when the gray threatened to engulf him again. He looked around slowly, his vision showing two of everything. He tried to remember how he ended up on the ground. Certainly someone must have snuck up and sapped him from behind. He reached up and carefully inspected the lump on the back of his head with his fingers. His knee felt a bit twisted, his hip stiff, and his arm had a large bleeding scratch on it.

Then he remembered the girl and the wall of air that pushed him. Flying? Certainly the knock on the head caused some type of delirium causing him to dream of flying backwards, pushed by some unseen force. He struggled to his feet and limped toward where he had seen her last. Maybe he could pick up her trail.

Then he saw her. She appeared out of the shadows and she carried the boy. Phil could see the tears running from her eyes. Forgetting his own injuries, he limped over to her and took the boy. Without any protest, she let him.

"He's dead, he's dead," she cried. The girl went to her knees. She buried her face in her hands and continued to cry.

Phil took the limp body and laid it down. He felt for a pulse and found nothing. He checked for breathing and still found nothing.

"Where's the guy? The one you're with?"

Roberta looked up. Dirt streaked her face and her eyes brimmed with tears.

"You know? The guy that's with you, the big one."

"Davy?"

That must be the one, Phil thought.

"Yeah, Davy. Where's he?"

"He's inside. In the hole. Something's wrong with him."

"Show me."

Roberta looked at Justin one more time. She didn't want to leave him.

"Now, please," Phil said. He felt danger. Weird tingles ran through his head. He reached up and scratched it.

Roberta got up and turned back toward where Phil had seen her coming out of the shadows. He reached for his flashlight as he followed her into the cave. Roberta disappeared into the dark as Phil fumbled it, trying to find the switch. When he turned it on, nothing happened. It, too, had shattered from the impact with the stone cliff. Already ahead of him in the main cave, Roberta paused for a moment, adjusting to the darkness then continued forward. Phil followed the currents of air left by her as she moved through the darkness. She stopped at the place she thought was near where she had taken Justin from only moments ago. Unable to see in the dark, Phil ran into her back.

"Down there," she said.

Phil reached out and found her arm. He slid his hand down past her elbow until he could follow her finger. He gently moved her out of the way and got down on his knees. He could feel the cooler lighter breeze coming from in front of him. He moved like a blind man feeling for the source of air. When he found the entrance to the interior cave, he reached in as far as he could, brushing the dirt with his fingers until he touched a fringe of cloth and a zipper. He clenched the fabric and pulled. It didn't move. He backed out and got on his knees beside Roberta.

"I can't see anything," he said. Strangely, he had an urge to crawl in the hole. He could smell the salsa dogs inside. Then he could see them, hot and steaming on a white porcelain counter. He tried to clear his head knowing that he was in a cave and there shouldn't be any restaurant. Then the vision expanded and he found himself looking down the long counter. Two city cops sat between him and the plate of food. In almost a dream like state, he got back down and started to worm his way through the passage.

***

The ulasiga had drawn back its activity knowing the Davy couldn't move on his own. The Phil had entered the cave, one more like the Davy, open to the ulasiga's touch. It lightly caressed the man's mind and quickly withdrew, anticipating another blast of feedback. Nothing came. Now the creature paused. Could it still reuse the Phil to bring more little men and keep the Davy? It probed the mind for a trigger that it could use. Inside the small cave, it had already circled the neck of the Davy, downloading the last of the memories. There wasn't much new since the last time, so the ulasiga let go and started to shut down the breathing and heart. Now it had an opportunity to have the food supply it required, plus the new memories, and it could use the Phil to bring more. A jail, a place where the Phil would bring what the image called criminals.

It would take the tired ulasiga time and energy to create and implant the idea. The ulasiga flowed further from its protected crack in the cave wall moving more of its body into the open. It had burned too much energy and it would take all it had to develop the Phil. It drew him in slowly, using memories and false feelings. When this new prey had come all the way inside, the ulasiga began to shut him down too, slowly and carefully. It only wanted to capture him, then download the memories. With one strand of its highly acidic, almost liquid body, hovering around the Davy's neck, it split more of its body off to circle the Phil's neck so it could play these new memories.

Greedy for the new memories, the ulasiga shifted to the lowest energy state it could and still hold the two in suspension. Then it began passing the new images through all of its cells, each sending waves to the next. Even the ones hovering over the Davy's neck saw the show. The ulasiga began to regain its strength while it watched and stored the memories. It knew the end came when the images became disjointed and unclear. When the last came through, the ulasiga reasserted control and began slowly completing the shutdown on the new food source and passing more of its dissolving juices to its arms that circled the neck of the Davy. As it did, it found the patterns on the Davy to be erratic and decaying. It focused on building images for the Phil for future use.

Without warning, searing pain jolted the ulasiga. It knew immediately that light had penetrated from somewhere and it burned. First the arms that hovered over the Davy and the Phil disintegrated under the light. They boiled and evaporated quickly with only a few residual drops landing on the victims. The acid, quickly neutralized, made small burns on their necks before disappearing completely. The creature released its mental hold on the two victims as it contracted. It tried to slip back into the crack and return to the safety of its lair while searching out the source of its pain. The pain grew in intensity confusing the ulasiga. It had never felt light traveling, only sudden and fixed. As it withdrew, it recognized the presence of the Roberta and fixed it as the source of the light. Like an animal attacking when hurt, the ulasiga assembled all of its remaining strength and snapped out at the Roberta, firing rapid pulses of the waves used to stop the heart and breathing. Then the pain stopped and all mental activity in the cave seemed to hover, suspended.

Roberta staggered with pain. A sharp jolt had hit her. It felt like her brain might split in two. She pulled back the flashlight and held her head. It felt like the last time the spider had entered her head. Again, she saw red.

The ulasiga felt a trickle of disjointed thought. Encouraged, it raced along the path of that energy preparing to send out a brain pattern that would drop the Roberta dead in its tracks. It never expected to find the path blocked by a familiar wave, a huge black pulse of feedback racing right back at it along the path of its attack. Following behind that wall of incoming feedback, the cells died at an incredible speed as the killing light trailed the wave. The ulasiga gripped the stone of the wall bracing against the tsunami about to engulf it. The light and the wave hit together, infiltrating every space where it tried to hide. The pain exploded into the very center of the creature.

The gelled form that was the ulasiga boiled as the light struck and what remained, an acidic liquid, ate into the sand. Small tendrils of white smoke rose from where the acid burned the dirt on the cave floor. The creature evaporated.

TWENTY-FOUR

"Hey! Davy! Mr. Police! Come on out of there. I need you to help Justin!" Roberta yelled as she waved the beam from Davy's flashlight around the small cave.

Phil slowly regained his senses and found himself in a small dark cave, lying against a body he couldn't see. In fact, all he could see was the flashlight racing around the hole. He caught a look at Davy's face when the light passed over it. Phil found Davy's shoulder in the dark and shook him. There was no response.

"Shine your light here!" he yelled to the girl.

Roberta put the beam on the policeman and saw he pointed to Davy. She moved the light to Davy's face and she saw that his eyes were closed.

"He's not breathing." he said.

She saw the policeman reach for Davy's neck and hold his hand there just below his jaw. She watched the policeman's face drop and his hand lift from Davy's neck. She heard him mumble something.

He turned toward Roberta, almost afraid to tell her; first the boy and now this guy. Even if he was the one that had snuck up behind him, Phil hated to lose anyone.

"He's dead."

Roberta moved the light back to Davy. He lay there with his eyes closed, face an ashen white in the artificial light just like her mother's had been. Streaks of dirt marked a trail of tears from his eyes across his cheeks. She thought of Justin outside looking much like Davy and then she thought of herself. Now she would be alone forever. She remembered their last talk in the park and how they had laughed. She remembered how he had made her feel important because of their mission. She raised a hand to her cheek where he had kissed her. She wouldn't get any of those things ever again.

She knew what had taken Davy from her, that cold ugly thing that had tried to get into her head. A monster had tickled her mind with its wet slimy fingers. She had tried to find it with Davy's flashlight as she shoved it away but it disappeared. It hadn't gone quietly. She could still feel an echo in her head, the last dying screams of the ulasiga. Looking around the cave again, her loss on her like a black, wet, quilt, she began to let her frustration flare into anger. Now Davy's stupid heart wouldn't beat. She pictured it in her mind, like the big red heart she had drawn for Valentine's Day. She squeezed it, but not too tight, then let it go. She did it again. This is what you're supposed to do, she scolded the image in her head. She then repeated the process, keeping time with her own. Beat you stupid headed heart, she urged. She heard Davy gasp. She found his face with her light as her mental picture dissipated.

His eyes opened and then his hand moved to shield them from the beam. Phil wasted little time in reaching out through the hole and grabbing the light from Roberta's hand.

"Are you alright?" he asked Davy.

Davy looked around wildly then turned toward the light, squinting at the brightness.

"Where's Protection? Where's Justin?"

"Outside. Come on, let's go. Let's get out of here."

Phil looked hard at Davy when he used the word 'protection' out of context. He filed it away. He wiggled out and then turned and grabbed Davy's hand. Davy kicked and pushed with his feet as hard as he could. He knew the other man did most of the work in dragging him out through the small hole. Together, the three staggered out of the cave holding each other up. When they finally broke into the light, Davy saw Justin lying on the ground outside. He rushed over to him with Roberta right behind and knelt by his side.

"He's dead, Davy. Poor Justin's dead," cried Roberta. She pictured little Justin's heart like she had Davy's but the image wouldn't form in her mind.

Then she began to cry again as the new grief enveloped her. Phil got down beside Davy and put his hand on his arm.

"Come on son. There's nothing you can do. We have to get you out of here and to a hospital."

Phil stood and tried to help Davy stand up. Davy shook off the policeman's grip.

"He's not dead!" yelled Davy.

Phil had seen this denial a hundred times and although he wanted to get off this mountain, he knew to let the man sit for a moment to allow reality to seep in.

Davy looked at Justin. He reached a large hand out and brushed the hair back from the tiny face. He could see the swelling and trails of dirt where tears had run creating lines of pain. Davy wished Justin hadn't died hurting. It had been Davy's job to save him. Davy sent him a final tickle and a ripple of love. With tears in his eyes, he stood, never taking his eyes off the tiny, still figure.

"Son, you have to lead the way. I'll carry the boy. Don't go too fast."

Davy just nodded his head. As he turned, he felt a wisp of feeling, a small whisper call to him. He whipped his head toward the cave, wondering if someone remained inside. The rush of mixed emotions weakened his knees. He didn't want to go back in there, not now, not ever. What was once a beautiful place now seemed like a nightmare. Then he realized the touch hadn't come from there. He looked down at Justin. He was alive! Davy closed his eyes to focus and flooded Justin with all the love and comfort he could muster, forcing it in with a thought. As Phil picked up the small child, he saw his eyes twitch underneath his eyelids, it wasn't much, just a flicker. He placed two fingers on the child's neck and this time he felt a thin unsteady pulse.

"Let's go!" said Phil. Without turning to see if they followed, Phil took off back down the hill toward the trail. He could hear the two behind him crashing through the brush.

Thankfully, the trail went downhill. Once he reached the path, he handed the boy off to Davy who began moving quickly down the trail with Roberta right on his heels, trying to look over his shoulder at the tiny figure of Justin. Phil followed them both, feeling twenty pounds lighter, blisters screaming, and his lungs burning.

When they entered the parking lot, Phil saw ten cop cars, some city, some state. An ambulance, lights rotating, sat parked next to a couple of Park Ranger jeeps and in the center of the parking lot, blades whirling, idled a Lifeflight helicopter. Davy and Roberta skidded to an immediate halt. Phil took Justin from them and almost ran to the chopper. Two EMT's stood beside the slowly rotating blades of their helicopter, hands in their pockets. When they saw Phil racing toward them, they went into action. Several cops converged on Phil while several others surrounded Davy and Roberta, who stood there dumb struck by all the lights and noise.

The medics grabbed Justin and set him on a gurney. Phil shouted what he knew about the boy's condition and the attendants carried him inside the helicopter, which lifted off moments later in a rush of wind and noise.

Phil watched it bank and turn toward the city. Children's Hospital would be its destination. After the helicopter disappeared from sight, he turned back toward his car. He looked up and saw Davy and Roberta, standing motionless, except for their heads, which turned in all directions trying to take in the whole scene. Several of his fellow patrolmen had taken up positions around the two while a couple others tried to ask him questions. He held up a finger, a wait sign, and he walked over to Davy and Roberta.

"Guys? Give me a minute, please?" he asked the cops.

They backed away without taking their eyes off the two, while Phil led Davy and Roberta to his car. He opened the door and waved his hand for them to get in the back. He could see the bewilderment and fear on their faces.

"I just want to talk to you two alone for a moment."

"But what about Justin?"

"He's on his way to the hospital. They'll take care of him there. Right now I have to talk to you."

Roberta and Davy looked at each other and then slid into the back seat. Phil closed the door behind them and then got in on the driver's side. He turned around to face them.

"You're Roberta and your name is Davy. Is that correct?"

They nodded their heads.

"Davy. Why'd you hit me up there by the cave?"

Davy and Roberta both looked at him.

"Davy didn't hit you, mister. He was in the cave. Remember?"

Now Phil looked confused. They were right.

"Okay, Roberta. Tell me what happened. How'd I get this?"

Phil moved his hand to the back of his head to show her.

"I don't know. You stood there and then you fell down. I got scared and ran into the cave."

Phil continued to rub the lump on his head as he mulled over what she said. He still didn't recall everything.

"And how did I get into the little cave?"

"You crawled. You went to get Davy."

"Why did you take Justin in there?"

Davy looked at the policeman for a moment. He didn't want to say. He was scared because he didn't believe in Protection anymore and he didn't want to get Mr. Harrington in trouble.

"Davy, I have to know. You have to tell me. It could be trouble if you don't."

"Tell him Davy. You have to."

"I was taking him to Protection."

Phil looked at him, wondering. Again, the misuse of the word protection.

"What? You were protecting him? From what? What happened to him? Start from the beginning."

Davy started slowly with his first trip up the trail and finding Protection. He told him about wanting to save abused children and being able to feel them. He explained about meeting Justin at the bus stop and about the woman that was beating Justin behind the school, although he didn't remember exactly where.

Davy gained speed as he went while Phil sat silently and listened, occasionally jotting down a few notes in case he needed to ask more questions later. Roberta would chime in when the story included her. Then Davy stopped abruptly at the part where he started up Black Trail.

"I don't remember much after that; just bits and pieces. I just felt something pull me in and I couldn't NOT do it. I saw Mr. Harrington but it wasn't really Mr. Harrington. Something went wrong and I couldn't fix it. Then Protection changed and it wasn't real and Mr. Harrington looked different and now Justin's hurt." Davy tried to suppress the tears but they flowed around his fingers.

"That's right! Something just took over Davy. He wouldn't talk to me or listen to me or anything," Roberta chimed in. "He even pushed me aside. I felt something try to pull me too, but I pushed it back."

Phil sat and looked at the two; adult bodies with children's minds. What did he believe? He believed that they saved the boy from a terrible beating. He believed they weren't the ones that hurt him and he believed they were harmless. The rest was too much to think about; a place called Protection inside a cave, a force pulling Davy in, seeing people that weren't there. Then again, he had been drawn to the cave, he had smelled the salsa dogs, and he had found himself inside without being really sure how he got there. Had something been in his head, something that directed him to the cave? He looked at the two sitting in the back seat.

"You said you could send tickles into kids?"

Davy looked down embarrassed.

"Try me."

Davy looked up at the policeman. He wasn't teasing him like others did and he didn't turn away like the other adults, making Davy look stupid. He looked like he wanted to believe. Davy sent a feeling through his eyes, light as a feather and goofy as his smile.

Phil saw the change in Davy's eyes as he concentrated. Phil had to smile at the absurdity of the whole thing. He almost laughed out loud at himself for succumbing to the gentle innocent face. How could he resist. But then Davy looked away and the feeling left. Phil had to wonder. Was it real? Had he done something? Phil shook it off.

Phil turned back toward the front, looking out through the front windshield. Some of the cars had left and the rest waited for his report. He turned back to them and noticed their heads together, whispering. They would say something and then giggle. Phil had to smile again.

"What are you two talking about?"

"Davy told me that when you were little, the kids called you 'Silly Philly'."

Roberta laughed again. Phil looked at her and then at Davy.

"How do you know that?" Phil asked.

Davy shrugged. "I know lots of things about you. All of a sudden, all this stuff was inside my head."

Phil gave up trying to understand.

"Let me go talk to the boss and then I think I'll take you home."

"Can we go see Justin?"

"I'll see."

Davy and Roberta sat in the car for a long time. One policeman came and gave them some bottled water.

"What happened?" Davy asked.

"What do you mean?"

"What happened up there, Roberta? I was lost and then I felt pain and all sorts of crazy stuff. I thought I was dead."

"The policeman said you were but I fixed it. I imagined your heart and I made it start again."

Davy looked at her, his eyes big and round and his jaw hanging open. "You can do that?"

"I think I can. You want to know a secret? I think I pushed that policeman into the wall that knocked him out."

"No!"

"Yes I did. He made me mad so I looked at him and wished hard and he flew backwards into the wall."

"Well don't tell anyone."

"I can remember better, too."

"I know. Now who is Betty going to call stupid?"

They both started to snicker again.

Phil returned and got in the car. He turned in his seat. "Davy, I'm going to come see you Monday and talk to you a little more. Roberta, Mrs. Anderson is going to talk to you. You have to tell her everything. Until we say it's okay, Davy, you can't go to the house and Roberta, you can't leave."

Davy and Roberta looked at each other. Roberta started to cry.

Phil quickly added, "Now, now, Roberta. It's all right. It's just for a day or two while we sort out the whole thing with Justin. I'm sure it will turn out fine."

Roberta looked back at Phil with her eyes still filled with tears.

"You sure?" she sniffed.

Phil didn't say anything. Instead he turned in his seat and started the car.

As he drove through town, Davy and Roberta huddled close together, whispering. Phil occasionally looked back at them. He couldn't hear what they were talking about and it didn't matter much to him. He saw them as two kids, harmless and well meaning.

Phil stood back and watched the uproar caused by the returning duo. Everyone joined in at the same time. Mrs. Anderson tried to scold Roberta while hugging her at the same time. Many from the group huddled around Davy asking all sorts of questions. A few even wandered over to Phil's patrol car, touching it carefully like some type of icon. Mrs. Anderson wanted to blame Davy for taking Roberta until Phil recounted the plausible parts of the story. Mrs. Anderson remained dubious.

The excitement continued until Mrs. Anderson clapped her hands sharply to quiet the group. "I'm sure we all have a lot of questions for Roberta but they will have to wait. It is late people, so off to your rooms and we will see her in the morning. Thank you officer for bringing her home. What do you say Roberta?"

"Thank you."

Phil saw a change in Roberta. She stood with her head down, not looking at anything but her feet. He felt a bit of sorrow at having to leave her there. She had shown so much love and concern for the boy. She had gotten Davy to respond when Phil thought he was dead. She had done something in the cave, while he had been ... been where? Salsa dogs? A restaurant in a cave? A jail? He felt like something foreign crawled in his head.

"Thank you, Roberta."

Roberta didn't move. Phil turned and walked toward his car then stopped and turned.

"I'll be back on Monday to talk to her some more."

"That'll be fine," said Mrs. Anderson.

There had been no word on the boy. As far as Phil knew, he hadn't regained consciousness yet. There had been no missing person's reports, nobody claiming to know him.

Phil dropped Davy off at his apartment with a gentle reminder to stay home until he came to see him on Monday.

TWENTY-FIVE

Phil went to the hospital on Sunday to see the boy. He stood in the doorway and saw the tiny form lying there under a sheet. He looked smaller than he had on the mountain. Phil saw that he barely made a dent in the big bed. Wires ran everywhere and electronic noise came from the monitors, beeping and humming, slowly. He looked like a baby Frankenstein being reanimated. The name on the door read Justin Doe. Still no parent or guardian identified. Phil walked over to the bed and looked down at the still figure. He watched for the rise and fall of his chest to indicate Justin was breathing. Only the tiniest movement of his cover gave it away. Justin's head had bandages wrapped all the way around and scratches showed on his face over the purple and yellowish bruises. Phil had carried the boy for miles down the mountain. He had been light as a feather. Now, looking at him lying there, helpless and hurt, Phil felt sad. Bad news for a cop. New rule number one: Never identify with the victim.

Squeaking footsteps caused Phil to reach up quickly and wipe a tear away. The nurse stood behind him.

"Will he be all right?"

"We don't know. He had a serious concussion, a bruised kidney, a cut liver, three cracked ribs, a broken wrist, a slight paralysis on the left side, although the doctor thinks it will be temporary, and he was a bit dehydrated."

"When can I talk to him?"

"That's what we all want to know. We don't know if there is any brain damage or when he will wake up. We had him in an induced coma for a while but we've stopped the drugs so we expect he will wake soon, maybe. There's really no time table for these types of injuries."

Phil watched as the nurse reached out and softly stroked Justin's cheek.

"No word on his parents?"

"No!"

Phil heard the anger as she spat the word and walked out. He understood. Phil looked back down at the small fragile boy under the sheets. For no reason at all, Phil tried to project love and warmth into him. What had Davy said? A tickle. Phil tried to send him a tickle. He shook his head at his sudden belief in magic, smiled and left the room. If he wanted magic, he thought, go get the magician.

***

Davy sat in his chair gazing out the window. Several times he closed his eyes and tried to feel the pull of Protection. He felt nothing anymore and Davy realized that it had been something else all along. He could recall the thoughts that had been forced into his head and could remember following them to their source. It had been some kind of monster, something bad. He recalled the intrusive mental fingers probing and it made Davy's skin bunch up and the tiny hairs on the back of his head rise. He had seen the thing in his mind but had been unable to resist because he had seen Protection and had wanted so much for it to be real.

"Stupid, stupid, stupid!" he said as he pounded his forehead with his fist. He thought of little Justin and wondered if he was alive. He thought he could feel him, but maybe he was just trying to fool himself again. "Stupid, stupid, stupid!"

He saw the police car pull up and Phil get out. Davy looked over his shoulder. It was Sunday wasn't it? The policeman wasn't supposed to come till tomorrow. Davy wondered just how stupid he had become. He met the policeman at the door.

"Come in, Sir," he said.

"You can call me Phil, Davy"

"Yes, sir, Mr. Phil," he replied. "Is it Monday?"

Phil saw the pale and nervous Davy with a strange red spot the size of a small orange on his forehead.

"No. It's Sunday," Phil replied.

Davy started hitting his forehead again, explaining the red spot, and saying, "Stupid, stupid, stupid."

Phil reached out and grabbed his arm. "Stop that Davy. You're not stupid."

"I am. I almost killed Justin. I fell for the trick and should have known. I don't even know the days!"

Phil watched as the anger built in Davy, the red creeping from his neck and rising.

"How would you like to go see Justin?" Phil asked.

Before Phil could react, Davy had him in a bear hug and jumped up and down. In spite of the jolting, Phil felt the grin on his own face. He tried to erase it as he separated from Davy.

"Calm down. This isn't official. We're just going to drop in on him. You have to promise to be quiet and not touch the boy, okay?"

Davy just stood there nodding his head up and down with a big smile covering his entire face.

"I'll show you the way," said Davy.

Phil looked at Davy. "Huh?"

"I'll show you the way to Justin."

"You know which hospital he's in?"

"No."

"How do you know where he is?"

"I can feel him a little, I think."

Phil decided to let Davy try.

Phil drove slowly and responded to Davy as he pointed in the general direction of the hospital.

"Turn, turn, turn," Davy would shout, pointing to a street going left or right. When the hospital appeared, large and ominous, Davy quietly pointed to it. "He's in there."

Once they went through the doors, Phil had to race to keep up with Davy as he went down corridors and halls, then up stairs, two and three at a bound. Phil found it hard to keep up because his legs were stiff and sore from yesterday's hike and his feet stung where bandages covered the blisters. Every stair jarred his still aching head.

Outside the door to Justin's room, Davy stopped and stood still. He turned to Phil and in a quiet whisper, asked if he could go in.

"We need to be quiet."

They both entered together. Phil had hoped to see Justin with his eyes open but the child lay flat on his back, pale and motionless.

"Davy? Can you send him a tickle like you told me? Let him know we're here?"

"Will it be okay?"

"I'm sure it's fine. Just a bit. Let him know he's safe."

Davy looked at the tiny figure on the bed, head wrapped, arm in a cast and wires running from everywhere. He looked so much smaller than yesterday. Davy could feel his own heart breaking, just sensing what sat inside the unconscious boy. Although some of the black had disappeared, there were many other feelings Davy recognized. Davy wasn't sure if he should disturb Justin at all until he felt the chill of loneliness. Along with that, he felt a confusing mix of pain and emptiness and a jagged pattern he didn't recognize. They came through heavy and metallic. Davy could feel the pain coming from Justin's wrist like foil on a filing and a thick throbbing from Justin's back. He also noticed the dullness of them as the medicine tried to mask it. At first, Davy sent just a little comfort to him and then reached out with his heart feeling for any difference. He felt no response. Davy pressed a little harder, closing his eyes to focus his mind. At first he felt no change in Justin and then quietly, softly, a tiny echo came to him. Davy smiled knowing that he had reached him. He gave Justin a full coating of all the love he had inside and then tickled him just a tiny bit because he knew making Justin giggle would hurt the boy.

Phil heard Davy chuckling. Phil felt himself smiling for no apparent reason. Phil felt a change, like sunshine tickling his insides. He looked at Justin and saw his eyes rolling under the lids and a smile forming on the pale boy's lips. He began coming around. Phil could hear the change in the machines tied to Justin. The pace of the whirring and beeping increased in frequency. Davy continued to lay the good feelings on the boy and received larger returns as the minutes passed. He felt the patterns within Justin change to match what Davy had come to recognize as the life force put out by children. He knew that Justin would wake up soon.

***

Mrs. Anderson sat at her desk and looked across at Roberta. Roberta sat quietly looking back with her normal innocent smile. Mrs. Anderson didn't know where to start. Lying on her desk sat the passbook with two missing passes. Beside them lay a small pile of splinters picked up from the broken door. Mrs. Anderson watched for any reaction from Roberta but Roberta just sat and smiled.

"Do you know what these are?"

"Passes!"

"Do you know where the missing ones are?"

"No."

Mrs. Anderson watched Roberta's face closely for signs of guilt, recognition, or shame. Roberta's eyes grew big and her mouth dropped open.

"I didn't take them!"

"You sure?"

"Nooooo."

"You didn't take these and leave the house?"

"Me? Why would I?" she asked.

Mrs. Anderson shook her head. Roberta couldn't remember yesterday. Now what?

"Why did you leave yesterday?"

"I just went out the door. I'm sorry."

"Did Davy come and get you?"

"No, but I saw him and so I walked with him up to the mountains."

"What about the little boy?"

"Little boy?"

Mrs. Anderson thought she saw a flicker of recognition flit across Roberta's face that quickly disappeared. She just knew Roberta wasn't capable of lying, she had probably forgot everything already. She'd never get any answers out of her.

"You remember the rules of the house don't you? No leaving without permission?"

"Yes, Mrs. Anderson. I'm sorry."

"Okay, you can go."

Roberta got up from the desk and went down the hall to her room. She went inside without even looking at the numbers on the door. She closed it quickly and sat on her bed. She looked in the mirror and smiled. Davy had been right. She clapped her hands, excited. Mrs. Anderson had believed her.

"Spaghetti!" she said.

***

Phil sat at his desk Monday morning filling out page after page of reports relating to the Davy and Roberta case. He tried to smooth over all of the unexplainable parts and anything that would point blame to Davy or Roberta. Although the two said Justin's injuries were caused by some woman, the fact that they had a hurt child with them couldn't just stay buried under the carpet. In Phil's mind it wasn't really kidnapping, child endangerment, assault on a police officer, or resisting arrest. He could see those two in front of a judge. It would turn out better if he could find a way to make it disappear. The phone on his desk rang and startled him out of the mental movie he ran.

"Officer Phil Maloney, may I help you?"

"Phil, they found the mother."

Phil banged his thigh getting up from his desk.

"Who? Where?"

"The townies got her Saturday morning. Found her drunk behind a school with a bloody club in her hand. She didn't remember much but what she claimed sounded pretty bogus. She said she was protecting her son from kidnappers until one of them threw her into the wall and knocked her out. When she asked about her son, we went to her house to check it out. We found a picture that matches your kid in the hospital. Didn't take J. Edgar to figure out the connection. Then we matched the blood on her club to her son. Child Services has been notified and she's facing the judge today."

"So she's the one that beat up the boy?"

"Yep! That head wound and bruise on his wrist, not to mention several on his back, all match up with the broom handle she had. She'll never get near him again."

"Thanks!"

Phil set down the phone and stared at the wall. You can't make sense out of what makes no sense, he thought. He looked at his watch. Rule number one; never miss lunch. Now maybe I can get a couple of dogs I can sit down and finish.

***

A hundred miles away, along the base of a boulder, a field mouse searched for the last remnants of pine nuts to hide away for the oncoming winter. Hundreds of feet below, the vibrations awakened a creature. If it had eyes, the ulasiga would have opened them.

About the Author

Glenn Oliver Parkhurst, author of *Bled Out*, takes his audience along on another gripping tale. He has used the mountains of Salt Lake City as the setting for this tale. The steep rocky trails, hiked often by Glenn, became the perfect place for this gripping thriller pitting man against monster. Follow Glenn on Twitter @oliverphurst and Facebook. Look for his next novel, Mad Men and Martyrs.

ALL THINGS THAT MATTER PRESS ™

FOR MORE INFORMATION ON TITLES AVAILABLE FROM
ALL THINGS THAT MATTER PRESS, GO TO
http://allthingsthatmatterpress.com
or contact us at
allthingsthatmatterpress@gmail.com